I0685913

What are people saying about
Murder of an Oil Heiress?

As a mystery this book works well but it is the character-isation where this book really comes in to play. The characters are extremely well written and every aspect of the way in which humans behave can be seen in this book. I felt I could picture each character perfectly and one of them is the most loathsome I have ever come across in a book
Bookaholic Blog – Wendy Jones

I love how POWER goes to people's heads and when it comes to family, you get greed, pride and all sorts of emotions coming to the fore. It's a fast paced adventure, I loved it.
Sue1958's review – Sue Ward

Tantalizing, fascinating, and exciting are all words that describe this book. Christie fans will love Candy Ann Little.
Allison Kohn

Murder of an Oil Heiress

By
Candy Ann Little

PUBLISHED BY:
Inknbeans Press

Cover art: YeSonDesign.

© 2013 Candy Ann Little and
Inknbeans Press

ISBN-13: 978-0615921082 (Inknbeans Press)

ISBN-10: 0615921086

All rights reserved.

Without limiting the rights under copyright reserved above, no part of this publication may be reproduced, stored in or introduced into a retrieval system, or transmitted, in any form, or by any means (electronic, mechanical, photocopying, recording, or otherwise) without the prior written permission of both the copyright owner and the above publisher of this book. This is a work of fiction. Names, characters, places, brands, media, and incidents are either the product of the author's imagination or are used fictitiously. The author acknowledges the trademarked status and trademark owners of various products referenced in this work of fiction, which have been used without permission. The publication/use of these trademarks is not authorized, associated with, or sponsored by the trademark owners.

Dedication

To Rosalie and Lori, without your support and encouragement this story would still just be a dream.

Chapter 1

The French doors squeaked as Mallory pushed them open, and the balmy Texas breeze embraced her as she walked onto the veranda. She watched the couples milling around the garden beneath her, their voices drifting on the wind. Normally she'd eavesdrop on such conversations, but tonight she didn't care. The idle gossip that she eagerly attended to held little amusement tonight. Nothing consumed her attention, except the large, blond cowboy. Tonight her plans were much bigger, around six feet two inches big, to be exact.

Her lips curved into a smile. She'd set the trap she'd been planning for months. Now, she waited for Joseph to step into it.

She took a sip of champagne from her half empty flute and gazed toward the sky. The waning crescent that hung in the darkness gave off little light, which, combined with the height of the balcony, would hide her rendezvous. Hearing footsteps behind her, she held her breath.

"It's a beautiful night." The deep voice didn't sound quite right.

Mallory turned to see David Preston standing in the doorway, blocking the path that Joseph should be taking.

"What are you doing here?" The disappointment made her voice sharp.

"I wanted to enjoy the view." His eyes traveled down her slinky, low cut dress, stopping at her breasts. "It certainly is the most impressive sight I've ever seen," he leered.

"You're drunk."

"C'mon, baby, you know me better than that." He stumbled forward, pinning her between his body and the balcony. "How about a little kiss? It's almost New Years."

She pushed at his chest but he stood there like granite. "Get away." She pushed harder.

"I see how you're gonna play it tonight." He bent his head toward her capturing her lips. "Son of a ..." He jerked his head up, wiping at his lip. "You bit me."

"I told you to leave me alone. I'm not kidding."

"Is there a problem out here?" Joe loomed in the doorway.

"No." Mallory said. "Nothing I can't handle."

"You were more than willing to be handled at the last party," David sneered.

"That was the last party."

"Whatever." David pushed passed Joseph, returning to the party inside.

"Are you sure you're all right?" Joe asked.

"Yes." Mallory fussed with the hairpins holding up her black tresses then pulled the spaghetti strap back up on her shoulder. "He's had a little too much to drink."

"Haven't we all?" Joe laughed.

"I guess so." He'd had more than enough to make her plan work. She'd made sure to add double shots of rum to his coke. After gathering herself together she asked, "Where's Sarah?"

"She went to bed." A dark look clouded his face.

"Are you two fighting again?" Her concern sounded real.

"Nothing major. She's not happy with my drinking."

"You're kidding?" Her blue eyes rolled up and thick, dark lashes framed the disgusted look. "You hardly ever drink, and this is a special occasion."

"That's what I told her." Joe watched her lips twist into a smile.

"You deserve to have a good time now and then." She held up her glass. "I could use another drink. This is warm." He was in the cage, now all she had to do was shut the door.

He took the glass. "I could use a refill too." He went to the bar and returned a few minutes later.

"Thank you." She took the new glass of champagne. "Can you close the doors? I don't want to get mauled again." She set the drink on a nearby table.

"You know, that dress might have something to do with it."

"Don't you like it?"

"Every guy in the room loves it. That's the problem."

"Why is that a problem?" Her tone took on an innocent sound that would rival Shirley Temple. "That's why I wore this dress." She stepped closer. "I wanted to impress every man in the room." Her sultry voice lowered seductively as she took another step. "This material is so smooth and silky." She slid her hands over her breasts and down to her hips.

Joe towered over her, watching her hands glide over the shiny black material.

"Do you want to feel it?" Her heart beat so fast that her hands were shaking. One more step and her breasts touched his muscular chest.

The contact shocked Joe and he jumped back. "No." His breath was jagged. "I mean, that wouldn't be appropriate." His words slurred slightly.

Mallory stepped back but kept eye contact. He wanted her. She could see it hidden deep down in those dark brown orbs. Putting her tongue between her bright red lips, she slowly moved it, leaving a wet trail that Joe watched hesitantly, hungrily.

Picking up her drink she took a long swallow, downing half the glass. "Ahh, that's better," she sighed.

"You weren't kidding about being thirsty." Joe laughed. He wanted to get back to the easy going, fun relationship they had always shared. Sure, they flirted sometimes but nothing serious, but for some reason tonight felt different – the connection stronger. Maybe the alcohol was affecting his thinking, or, perhaps, the fact that it was the beginning of a New Year was playing havoc with his body. Either way, he couldn't let these feelings go to his head.

"I never kid when I want something." Like a lioness she stalked forward. The voices inside rose in unison as they counted down the last seconds of 2013, and when the cheers finally erupted, she stood next to him. "Are you going to kiss me? It is a new year."

"Sure." He bent to give her a peck on the cheek. After all, the tradition did call for a smooch. Since Sarah had left the party, he had no one, and Mallory sure was a fine replacement.

However, she turned her head and captured his lower lip with her teeth, sucking it into her mouth. The kiss was long and passionate. She moved closer, positioning herself tight against him.

He tried to pull away but she touched his lips again with her mouth, sparking a desire that reached all the way to his toes. She dropped her glass, the shattering sound mingling with his moans. Her hands wound around his neck. Her fingers entangled in his thick hair.

"I love the length of your hair," she whispered.

The moment apart helped clear his foggy head. "Mallory, we can't." He started to pull away.

She inched closer, knocking him off balance and plastering him against the closed door. The slight angle made it easy for her to straddle his legs. "You never did feel my dress." Grabbing his hand she placed it on her breast.

He groaned, "Mallory."

He still sounded unsure, so she knocked his drink out of his other hand and placed it on the other breast. "See, doesn't it feel nice?" After placing her fingers on top of his, she slowly moved his hands down the trail she'd shown him earlier. "Smooth?" she whispered, huskily.

"Yes." Desire flared in his eyes. Their hands continued down her body.

"Silky?" She could hardly restrain the passion he produced.

"Oh, yes," he groaned. When she let go of his hands, he continued further down on his own. Reaching behind, he pulled her butt closer until she straddled him. He covered her scream of pleasure with a hard kiss.

With her body pressed tight against his and the liquor muddling his thoughts, he let go of all doubts. Kissing her with every ounce of passion his body possessed. She moaned and withered beneath his touch. He worried that he was going to hurt her but she seemed to respond to his passion with a viciousness of her own. He could never be this rough with, Sarah. His wife was much too fragile to make love like this.

Thoughts of Sarah splashed across him like cold water. He stopped kissing Mallory, abruptly pushing her away from him. "We can't do this."

She saw the desire being replaced with deter-mination, and knew better than to fight it. He may be a little on the slow side but had a stubborn streak wider than the Texas sky.

"I'm sorry, Mallory." He raked his fingers through his hair then jerked open the door.

Mallory allowed the breeze to cool her body. It wouldn't help her temper, though. "I was so close this time." She stomped her foot. He wanted her, she'd felt it. So why didn't he succumb to her wiles?

Then determination kicked in. He was so very close to giving in this time. She ran through the crowd smiling, waving and wishing people a Happy New Year on her way to the door.

The crowd must have slowed Joseph also because he was just going out the door as she neared it. Leaning against the wall she fiddled with her heel, loosening it. Yanking open the door, she pretended to hurry down the hall. "Joseph, wait."

He turned just as she fell to the floor.

"Mallory are you okay?" He knelt down.

She started laughing. "Stupid heel broke." She held up the four inch black spike. "I spent two hundred dollars on these and they break the first time I wear them."

He started laughing too. "I don't see how you women can even walk in those things."

"You learn."

"Why don't they make them better so they don't fall apart? I mean, my boots stay together for years before I wear them down."

"Don't worry about it. I have lots of shoes I've bought and never worn at all."

"You rich folk. It must be nice." The truth cut into his playfulness.

"Sometimes." She started laughing again. "Okay, all the time." She tried to struggle to her feet but slipped.

"Although," she slurred her words on purpose, "there are times when being rich isn't all that great."

"Like when?" He slipped his arm around her waist and helped her up.

"When paying taxes. The more money you have the more taxes you pay."

"Okay, that's a good point." Joe wasn't about to argue. But one point still remained, the Dillinghams had more money to spend in a given month than he could earn in a lifetime.

She leaned against him to steady herself. "I could hardly walk straight before my heel broke. Now how am I going to make it to my room?" She held the heel up.

He took it. "I can fix that for you. A little super glue and it'll be good as new."

"Don't trouble yourself." She waved the offer away.

"It's no trouble, really. Besides if you spent that much money on them you should get more than one use out of them."

"Okay, mister handyman, if you help me to my room I'll let you fix my shoe." As they walked down the hall she kept stumbling into him, careful to make it look like an accident. With her drinking so much and now uneven heels, the situation was perfect for some bumping and stumbling.

Joe stopped and looked down the long hall. Sarah was in their room, waiting. Mallory's room was located upstairs. He didn't know if he could control himself again. He had to keep a distance because his body still felt weak from the last encounter.

"I promise to keep my hands to myself." She held up two fingers on her right hand. "Scout's honor."

"It was just as much my fault." He looked down at the floor.

"Look, we've both had a lot to drink. Nothing happened and Sarah doesn't have to know."

He looked into her eyes. They shined like sapphires. "I don't like keeping secrets from her but with all we've been going through lately I'm not sure she'd understand."

"Then don't say anything. I won't say anything. And nobody saw us." She crossed her heart with her index finger. "I promise not to say a word." She put her arm around his bulky shoulders. "Now, be a gallant knight and help me hobble to my room."

"All right." With his arm around her tiny waist they limped up the stairs.

After reaching her door he let his arm fall to his side. "Goodnight, Mallory." He sounded awkward. He wondered if they could ever get past that kiss, since it wasn't going to be easy to forget passion like that.

"What are you thinking about?" Mallory opened her door.

"Nothing," he lied.

"I just have one more favor to ask." She held up her finger.

His bushy blond brows rose and skepticism showed in his eyes.

"Just a tiny little favor, please." She made an inch space with her finger and thumb. "I'm too drunk to get my sandals undone. Can you undo them for me?"

"I'm not sure I can." He saw the pleading look and pouting lips. "All right, I'll try." Why did he always seem to fall for that look?

Mallory stumbled over to her bed, sitting on the edge. After Joseph knelt down, she lifted her foot into his hands. The soft fabric of her dress brushed across his hand. He froze as he remembered the feel of it hot against her body.

He fumbled a few times before finally getting the tiny metal buckle undone. "How in the heck did you get these on?"

"Well, for one my hands aren't as big as yours. And, two," she held up two fingers, "I wasn't drunk."

They both laughed as the sandal fell to the floor. She shifted on the bed, placing her other foot in his hand and hiking her dress up to show more of her leg. Holding it high enough to give him a good view all the way up to her underwear, if she'd had any on.

Joe managed to divert his attention entirely on the shoe, fighting the urge to look up. However, when her bare foot started rubbing against his leg, he glanced up, lingering a few seconds too long on the forbidden zone.

"Mallory." He snapped, angry that the pounding blood was rushing to parts that it shouldn't.

"Sorry. I have an itch." She bent over and started scratching her foot, moaning in pleasure. "That feels so good." The fabric that had hugged her curves all night fell away giving him full view of her breasts.

His hands froze. He didn't dare move a muscle. Didn't even blink. He had to think, had to get away. His mind started spinning. He really did drink too much. The booze was messing with his head and Mallory seemed to be messing with everything else.

Suddenly, her hand settled on the sandal. She quickly unbuckled the strap, the shoe hit the floor. "Do you know what I love most about your name, Joseph Barnes?" She slid closer to the end of the bed.

"What?" For having drank so much, his throat felt awful dry.

"Your surname means works in a barn."

"So?" He wanted to ask what was so great about that, but couldn't string that many words together.

"I've come to find that working men are so much better with their hands." Her voice dipped low, seductive. "And their tools."

Her breasts pressed closer to his face. He had to get away. Had to stop this nonsense. "I should be going." He heard the words over his pounding heart.

Before he could move, she wrapped both legs around his waist. "Before you go, I should give you something for helping me." She pressed closer. Her breasts felt like they were on fire.

"I ... I don't need anything." His head spun out of control.

"But every maiden gives her knight something to remember her by." She leaned even closer.

"But I'm not ..." Her breasts were in his face. He felt the warmth of them through the thin, cool cloth. How could something be so hot and cold at the same time? So sweet, and yet bitter? Be wrong, yet feel right?

He turned his head but found her breasts there. They were like magnets following his mouth. He knotted his hands into fists and kept them at his sides. He turned his head again and tried to get up, but her legs were like a vise clamped onto him, gripping him in place. "No! No! No!" The word rolled around his mind, spilling out of his mouth.

"Yes! Yes! Yes!" Mallory echoed as if in ecstasy. After ripping the strap on one side of her dress, she arched her back enough to thrust the bare breast even further into his face.

This time there was no material between his mouth and her flesh. Every nerve tingled in his body. He had no control. No choice. He reached out with his tongue and lapped at the pink morsel taunting him.

Mallory screamed with pleasure as he kissed her soft skin.

His hands finally came up to enjoy the activities. He ripped the other strap and both breasts fell, full and naked before his eyes. "We really shouldn't be doing this," he panted. Although his head said no, the other parts of his body were screaming yes!

"Who cares." Her voice was husky, thick with desire.

How long had it been since a woman had made him feel this way? How long since his wife had wanted him? His hands kneaded the soft flesh. His lips tasted the ripe spots.

Mallory inched closer and closer, moaning with each touch. Then she slipped off the end of the bed and fell right into his lap. They laughed for a moment, sitting face to face. If he were going to stop, this would be the right time.

But he didn't stop. He kissed her lips, those full ripe lips that tasted like wild cherries and -surrendered to the reckless passion raging through his body. Lips on lips. Lips on flesh, and hands roaming everywhere. The desire consumed them and couldn't be tamed.

Mallory stopped, panting for air.

His breathing came in uneven spurts too, but he couldn't quench this feeling on his own. He needed her. Grabbing her head, he attacked her lips once again.

"I need ... to shut the ... door," she managed to gasp between kisses. She wiggled out of his lap, kissing him with each move. As she stood, her naked breasts rubbed against his face one more time, but she quickly withdrew before he could touch them.

"Come here." He tried to pull her back into his lap.

"In a minute." She stood, smiling down at him. The longing in his eyes told her he needed release and she knew just how to please him. She'd been waiting for this moment for years.

He looked up. The black evening gown hung from her waist down and her creamy skin glistened from the waist up. He couldn't reach the top half so he grabbed the hem of her dress.

"What are you doing?" She couldn't take another step.

"I said come here." He yanked her back down. She fell to her knees and he captured her mouth again. He maneuvered his body so that they both were on their knees. Wrapping his arms around her, he crushed her to his chest with a grip so strong a pro wrestler wouldn't have been able to escape.

Her hands felt every muscle growing taut as they kissed and played. He was taking control and that was fine, but she had this night planned and had one more thing to do. "I really have to get ..."

He silenced her with a bone-crushing kiss. "I don't care about the door." His hands flowed over her body.

She kissed him back. Her hands fumbled with his buttons, they were too small, or the passion too strong. She couldn't control herself anymore, so she ripped his shirt open, allowing her silky breasts to brush against his chiseled chest. "Oh," she gasped.

He pressed her closer to the bed, trying to find the hem of her dress and pull it up, but it had entangled under her knees. Her kisses seared the skin on his chest and the passion consuming him made the thought processes hard. He had to have her right now. He wanted to see, feel, and taste her whole body. He was tired of feeling the fabric, he wanted bare skin, needed to explore other parts of her body.

His large hands grabbed the thin material and with another rip the gown lay in a pool of black silk around Mallory's knees. Finally, his hands and lips devoured the rest of her naked body. "That's much better," he whispered.

"Oh, yes." She forgot about the door, her plans and even her name. This man knew how to please a woman. She liked him taking charge. He'd always been that kind of man. Three years she'd waited, three years of planning and scheming that had never seemed to work. Tonight was payday. And, he'd most definitely been worth the wait.

The pleasure tingling through her was stronger than she wanted. His hands produced feelings she'd never felt before. She tried breaking free of his grasp one more time but he locked her in place with one arm while the other hand roamed south. "Joe, not yet." But her body shook with pleasure before she could stop him.

"Yes. Now." His voice raged strong, hard, just like his body, while his fingers rubbed at her delicate spot.

Her lips found his, the kiss so fierce that she tasted blood. His mouth and hands commanded a response from her body. She willingly gave in to the delight and screamed as the pleasure peaked, then flowed out of her. Breathless, she fell against the bed.

He let her have a minute to savor the feeling, but not long. He wasn't done yet. She took the moment to try and stand up. His arms wrapped back around her again. "Where do you think you're going?"

"I'll only be gone a few seconds." She pointed to the door. "I really don't want someone to walk by and see us."

"All right, go," he sighed. She was right. With the party breaking up anyone could waltz down the hall. He playfully patted her butt as she stood. "Do you ever wear underwear?" His knees were aching so he shifted into a sitting position, leaning against the bed.

"Sure." She closed and locked the door then made a detour to her closet.

His eyes followed her every movement. He had to admit her beauty when clothed, but fully naked she was even more glorious.

After fumbling around, she found what she wanted. "Here" She tossed a box across the room.

"Edible underwear?" He arched a bushy brow over his dark eyes.

"The only kind I wear." She stopped in front of him, smiling down at him. "I'll even let you put them on me." She leaned down, her breasts dangling in front of his mouth. "Of course, taking them off is more fun."

He jumped up, almost knocking her over. With one arm he scooped her up and tossed her onto the bed where she sprawled out before him. "I'll put them on," he ripped the box open with his teeth, "and take them off," he growled.

"Whatever you say, Joseph." Her plan was in motion and she didn't care who took control. "You can do whatever you want."

Chapter 2

Joe slowly opened his eyes, but a hammer pounding in his head made him close them again. He lay there a few minutes, trying to remember why his head hurt so much. Putting a hand to his forehead, he sat up, but the movement only made the pounding worse.

As his eyes adjusted to the light, he looked around the room, realizing this wasn't his bedroom. Too many questions rolled around his brain. Why couldn't he recall anything about last night?

His head hurt, his stomach ached and he seemed to be suffering from amnesia. "What's going on?" he mumbled. As he became more awake, details started emerging from the fog that clouded his brain. He remembered the party, and drinking. That would explain why he felt so sick – a hangover.

Then bits and pieces of the fight with Sarah emerged. During the last few months they'd done nothing but fight… he didn't even know why, most of the time. Sarah's mood swings left him puzzled, because she was normally so mild tempered. Why did everything he say and do seem so wrong, lately?

So, that explained being in a different bedroom. He tried placing the red bedspread but couldn't recall a guestroom that had been done in red. Whenever he slept apart from Sarah, he usually stayed in a room that had neutral tones. But with so many guests staying overnight maybe that room had already been taken.

As his memory cleared even more, other flashes hit him like a sledgehammer. The churning in his stomach was no longer from the after effects of alcohol, but guilt. "What have I done?" He shook his head, trying to erase the pictures unfolding before his mind's eye. Maybe it was just a dream. He'd certainly had pornographic dreams before. That had to be it, a bad dream. A really, really bad dream.

He tossed the blanket away, noticing his nakedness. *This isn't a good sign*, he thought. Just then Mallory came out of the bathroom, a roll of steam billowing out when she opened the door.

"I see you're finally up, sleepy head." Her black hair hung in wet layers that brushed the top of her shoulders. The red and gold Chinese robe flowed behind her as she walked toward the bed.

Joseph quickly pulled the covers back over his lower parts.

"Don't be shy now, darling." She stopped directly in front of him. "I did more than look last night." Her voice was low, sexy and tempting. "I smelled, touched and tasted you." The robe hung open at the top, and a split showed her bare leg. "Don't you remember?"

"No." His stomach knotted tighter. He couldn't have... he wouldn't have slept with anyone else, especially his sister-in-law. "That can't be true."

"How about I refresh your memory." She climbed onto the bed, inching closer to him. He could smell the jasmine in her hair. The belt loosened around her waist and the top opened even more. He tried not to look but couldn't help it.

She straddled him. "Does this ring any bells?" Untying the belt she held open her robe. Images from the night before crashed into his mind.

"No." He scooted back on the bed. "Mallory, stop it."

"I assume last night is coming back to you." She smiled and leaned closer, her face an inch away from his. "Good. I want you to remember every single detail." Her breath smelled of mint.

"Mal ..." Her lips devoured his, breaking off his protest. The kiss was unexpected, hard and hungry. Too stunned, at first to do anything, it took a few seconds for his brain to kick into action.

She broke away from him and smiled. "I want to relive each and every minute." Sitting up she inched closer while letting her shoulders slip out of the robe. "We can start here." She pushed her naked breasts closer to him. "Remember how good they felt? How you touched me?"

He sat there, staring, while mental pictures of Mallory mixed with ones of Sarah causing confusion and a deep regret.

"What a way to start off a New Year." Her fingers brushed through his hair. She started pulling his head closer to her breasts. "Do it again, baby."

The daze finally wore off and he grabbed her wrists, jerking her hands away. "Mallory, no." He tossed her off him and jumped out of the bed. "Whatever happened last night isn't going to happen again." The authoritative tone lost some of its sway, as he stood there naked.

One look told her everything she wanted to know. He was tempted. "You started out saying no last night." She slid off the bed. "But, ended up giving in." She stepped closer. "Over and over and over again." She brushed up against him.

"You're confusing me. I can't think." He moved away. "Where are my clothes?"

"All over the place." She waved her hand around the large room. "Your guess is as good as mine."

He walked to the end of the bed noticing a pile of clothes. Picking them up, he found his shirt with a torn black dress. He looked at Mallory, alarm ringing in his head. Had he done this?

She smiled seductively. "Don't worry about it. I damaged some of your stuff too."

"This can't be happening." He looked around for the rest of his clothes. "Where are my pants?" He found them under the bed. Thrusting a leg into the hole, he lost his balance and almost fell over. He grabbed the bedpost to steady himself.

"Sarah's going to kill me." The thought of his sweet, innocent wife knowing what a scumbag he truly was made him feel sicker than the hangover.

"Joseph, quit being such a baby." Mallory pulled her robe on, tying the belt firmly around her waist. Walking closer, she slapped him. "Get a hold of yourself."

"What's that for?" He yelled.

"You're getting hysterical. They do that in the movies."

"This isn't a movie. It's my life."

"It's my life too."

"She'll never forgive me." His chest constricted at the thought of losing Sarah, and he had to fight back tears. He couldn't understand how this all had happened. Why had he done this? "I want to know what happened last night." With his pants buttoned he faced her.

Mallory arched a perfectly tapered brow.

"Not the sex part. I get that." He ran a jittery hand through his hair. "How did I get from a party downstairs up to your bedroom?"

"You walked." Her indifferent tone irritated him.

"Mallory, stop it," he yelled. "This isn't a game."

"Of course not. We played all the games last night." She walked to the stand next to the bed and picked up a pack of cigarettes. "Apparently you played too much, because you aren't any fun this morning."

The woman was making his headache even bigger. Did she have any clue what was at stake for him?

Did she even care? "I don't care what happened or how I got here, as long as it never happens again." He thrust his arm into the shirt.

"You make it sound like I drugged you. Or forced you up here." She feigned shock and hurt.

Sure, she may have put double shots of alcohol in his drinks, and since he didn't usually drink much, the alcohol hit him hard, but she didn't drug him. And, she certainly didn't force him. Maybe, she did coerce him at first. However, he had the power to walk away, but he hadn't. He'd stayed, and enjoyed every second of it.

"That's not what I meant." He tried finding the buttons but none was left. "I don't know what I was thinking. I don't remember much."

"You'd been drinking." She blew out a stream of smoke. "So had I. We both had too much to drink and ended up sleeping together. I'm sure that, as your hangover subsides, your memory will return."

"I don't care about remembering." He looked around for his shoes. "I'm going to forget this ever happened." He picked up one loafer.

"Too bad. It was the most incredible night of my life." She smiled. "By the way you acted, I'm sure it was the best sex you've ever had."

"Stop talking like that." He looked for his other shoe. "Do you have any idea what we've done?"

"Oh, yes." She smiled as she stomped out the cigarette. "We had fun. Something you can't get with my sister."

"Shut up. Don't you dare say a word about Sarah."

"Come on, you know it's true. She's stiffer than the pipes on the oil rig."

He dropped the shoe and ran across the room, grabbing her by the shoulders. "I said *shut up!*"

Throwing her head back, she laughed. "Doting little Sarah is boring you out of your mind, whereas I made you scream with pleasure."

His hands tightened and he started shaking her like a rag doll. "Don't ever say that again." The words came through clenched teeth. He threw her on the bed. "This will never happen again."

"We'll see."

He picked up his shoe again and headed to the door without looking back.

"Happy New Year, darling." Her wicked laughter echoed behind him as he walked down the hall.

By the time Joe got showered and went to the dining hall for breakfast, he thought he'd be the only one there, since most of the family usually got up early. However, the whole gang was seated at the long table when he walked in.

"Good morning, Joe." Richard Dillingham sat at the head of the table. His thick gray hair, combed into place, matched his short beard, and his hazel eyes were as sharp and attentive as ever, watching from under bushy brows. He looked every bit the millionaire oil man that he was.

He'd tucked his usual white dress shirt into blue jeans, leaving the first three buttons undone. A blue handkerchief had been tied around his neck, and brown cowboy boots protected his feet.

"Morning, sir." Joe avoided eye contact and went to the sideboard loaded with an array of breakfast dishes. Since his stomach was still rolling, he only got a cup of coffee then took a seat next to Sarah.

"Aren't you hungry?" she asked. "Usually you eat enough for three people."

"I'm not feeling too well this morning." Joe looked into her almond shaped eyes. Love and trust resided there, but how long would those feelings still belong to him? He'd betrayed her.

"You must have one heck of a hangover," Robert teased him. "You sure had a lot to drink at the party." Although he liked his brother-in-law well enough, his protective nature had surfaced since he'd married his baby sister.

"I didn't have all that much," he defended. "It just seemed to hit me hard for some reason."

"You didn't come to bed at all?" Sarah questioned.

Joe stiffened. His brain scrambled for an excuse. "I, umm, I didn't want to wake you so I used a guest-room." It's not like he hadn't done that before. He'd spent several nights in one, after fights. Or at times, when Sarah complained about his snoring, he'd let her have their room and go to a guest-room.

"Which room?"

Did she know? She didn't usually ask questions like this. "I'm not really sure. It wasn't my usual one."

"You make it sound like you sleep in the guest room all the time." The slight rise in her soft tone was the first indication that she was upset. Stabbing her eggs hard with her fork was the second. "You hardly ever sleep in another room. In fact, in the three years we've been married, you've only slept away from me a handful of times."

"I didn't mean I do it all the time." Joe sighed and sipped his coffee. "But I normally stay in the room across the hall."

"So where did you end up?" Robert asked.

"In a room upstairs."

"Why all the way up there?" Richard asked, curious now.

"Well." Joe cleared his throat. "I figured with so many guests spending the night that all the lower guestrooms would be taken."

"Good point." Richard admitted. "But we didn't have that many guests stay overnight this year."

"Wasn't that the most wonderful party ever?" Mallory sashayed into the room, looking bold in a black and white pants suit.

"Happy New Year." Richard smiled. "What has you in such a good mood?"

"Nothing much. I just had the best time of my life last night." She grabbed a plate, adding ham, eggs, and hash browns. "I love starting the New Year off with a bang." Walking over to the table, she met Joe's eyes and winked.

He stiffened.

"Wow, Mallory, what's gotten into you?" Robert looked at her plate. "You usually have dry toast for breakfast."

"I'm famished this morning." She smiled at Joe.

"I didn't see you after the ball dropped," Richard commented.

"No, I went to bed early. That David Preston kept bothering me."

"When are you going to quit leading that boy on?" Richard asked. "You've got him hopping around after you like a horn toad."

"Yeah," Sarah sighed. "You didn't mind him bothering you at the last party."

"He wasn't dating someone else before." She took a forkful of eggs. "Don't you just hate cheaters?" She looked at Joe.

He stood. "I think I'm going to see if the game has started." The air seemed to be getting thinner than on the top of a mountain. His queasy stomach knotted.

"It's only ten o'clock," Robert observed. "I don't think the games start for a few more hours."

"Then I'll watch the parade. I just don't feel like eating." If Mallory smiled, winked or made another innuendo, he was going to choke her.

"Joe, can we talk?" Sarah stood in the doorway of the large family room, her hands folded in front of her. She looked like a child waiting to enter the principal's office.

"Sure." He pressed the mute button on the remote.

Sarah took a deep breath, then ran her hands up and down her arms. The cashmere sweater felt soft, and its sage green hue complimented her hazel eyes and light skin tone. Licking her soft pink lips, she walked to the couch, hesitantly sitting next to her husband.

Joe's hands started sweating. He rubbed them against his blue jeans. He felt a hammer hitting his heart. *This is it*, he thought. Had Mallory told her already? Would Sarah even give him a chance to explain? To apologize. *How could I have been so stupid*? The thought kept repeating, but he still had no answer.

How am I going to explain this, he wondered? He'd thought of nothing else for the last two hours and

Murder of an Oil Heiress

still he didn't have the right words. He reached out taking her hand, the softness of her skin, the warmth and tenderness flowed through him.

"I have something I need to tell you." She finally found her voice. "I don't know where to start." She squeezed his hand.

He sat there waiting, his heart pounding so hard he wasn't sure he'd be able to hear her words. Thousands of tiny pins pricked along his spine, arms and heart.

"Sarah, I'm sorry. I'm so, so sorry. But, please don't let this be the end of us. I'll change. I'll stop drinking. I'll do anything you want me to." He swallowed back tears and heard his voice crack.

"What on earth are you talking about?" Sarah stared at him, confusion clouding her eyes. "Oh, honey, this isn't about last night." She brushed her fingers through his hair, smoothing back the long locks. "I'm the one that should be apologizing."

"For what?"

"I didn't mean to get so angry. I really wasn't feeling well, that's why I turned in early. And, I know you were just unwinding and trying to have some fun. I shouldn't have begrudged that."

"So this isn't about last night?" He brought her hand to his mouth, placing kisses on her palm.

"No." She pulled her hand away. "It's something else."

What else could be so important? Then a thought struck him louder than a gong. It didn't matter what she had to say. After he told her what happened between him and Mallory, their marriage would be over. She'd divorce him quicker than a jackrabbit hopping from the clutches of a coyote.

Should he even tell her? What if he just kept it a secret? Mallory wouldn't say anything. Surely, she didn't want her sister to know that she'd had sex with her husband. Her father would be irate. Not only could it cost Mallory her reputation in the family, it could very well cost her the coveted position in the oil business.

He'd gone back and forth on the issue. He didn't want to break his wife's heart, but he couldn't live with a secret this big. His only option was to tell her and throw himself on her mercy.

"Sarah, there's something I must tell you." His voice quivered with each word.

"Let me go first," she pleaded. "I've been trying to tell you for a long time and every time I try, I seem to back down." She tucked some brown hair behind her ear and licked her dry lips. "I need to get it out before I lose my courage again."

"Okay." He'd always lived by the gentleman's rule, 'ladies first.' Plus, he wasn't in a hurry.

Sarah stood, pacing the floor, looking for courage. "I don't know how to say this so I'm just going to say it." She looked Joe in the eyes. "I'm pregnant."

"What?" he whispered, unable to say anything. The word tried registering in his brain but he couldn't quite grasp the meaning. "You mean like *a baby*?"

"Exactly." She smiled at the confused look on his face. His strong, wide features took on the innocence of a little boy. For a few seconds she glimpsed the child in him, the part of him that made her fall head over heels in love.

"I'm going to be a dad?" He sat, dazed.

"Yes." She sat back down. "Are you okay with this? I know we weren't planning on kids quite this soon."

"A baby." His world tipped slightly. "I'm going to be a dad." He felt a rush unlike anything he'd ever felt before. A mix of joy and dread.

Sarah took his hand. "You're going to make a terrific dad."

"I will?" He didn't grasp the concept yet.

"Yes." She smiled, her purity of heart shining through, her faith and love radiating from her eyes. She said nothing else, just waited for him to absorb the news.

Her words hit him one at a time. Finally wrapping his mind around the fact, he asked. "When is she due?"

"She?" Her soft brow arched. "In June."

"June." He ran a quick mental calculation. "That means you're four months along." He paused. "Why didn't you tell me sooner?"

Sarah inhaled deeply and stood. "I told you I tried and couldn't." Her eyes misted up.

"Did you think I'd be that upset?"

"No." She walked over to the fireplace, staring up at the large framed painting of a woman. Her mother had been a stunning beauty. Dark black hair softly swept past her shoulders and eyes bluer than the Texas sky, reverently watched over her family. "The truth is it took me a while to accept this. I've been seeing a therapist for the last few months."

Joe stood, quietly coming to stand behind her. "Aren't you happy about the baby?"

"It's complicated." A tear rolled down her cheek. "I'm scared."

His large arms encircled her waist and he rested his chin on top of her head, looking at the painting. "You're afraid you might die in childbirth like your mother?"

"Yes," she whispered.

Joe just held her and didn't say anything. What could he say? He felt scared at the thought of losing Sarah too. What would he do if anything happened to her? So many questions and doubts rolled around that he started feeling apprehensive about the baby.

"Have you thought about having an abortion?"

"No." She turned around so quickly, he almost lost his balance. "Not for a minute. This baby is a part of you and a part of me. I could never kill it."

"I don't want to lose you."

"My mother gave up her life so that I could live." She turned back to look at the woman who'd given her life. "My entire life, I've felt an enormous amount of guilt over causing her death." She laid her hand across her abdomen. "Now I understand how she felt. I'd give my life willingly to save our baby."

"I guess I'm more selfish than you." Joe hugged her close. "I'm not willing to give you up."

"Oh, sweetheart, you don't have to worry. The doctor said everything is fine. My blood pressure is a little high, but other than that I'm healthy."

Joe pulled back, staring into her eyes. "Your blood pressure is too high?"

"It's common with mothers to be. I just need to take it easy and not have too much stress." Lifting up on tiptoes, she placed a light kiss on his lips. "It's no big deal."

"Take it easy and no stress." Joe repeated to himself. He couldn't tell her now. He not only had a wife to protect, but a baby too. How had his life become so complicated?

Sarah snuggled into his embrace, laying her head on his chest. "Now, what did you want to tell me?"

Joe hesitated a moment. "Nothing important." He bent his head close to her ear, whispering, "I love you, Sarah, more than anything."

"I love you too."

Chapter 3

Everyone gathered in the parlor, waiting until dinner was ready to be served. The Dillinghams always ate at precisely six o'clock. Several guests, still present from the previous night, mingled with the family, having drinks and talking business, or discussing the outcome of the football games.

Mallory stood in a group of several men, one of whom was the accountant for Dillingham Oil, William Moss. The conversation revolved around business only, as Mallory wouldn't allow personal information to be used in the presence of business partners.

Sarah stood off in a corner of the room, chatting with a neighbor, who'd been like a substitute mother to her, while Richard's deep voice could be heard recounting the plays of the game.

Joe stood in the doorway, watching the room. His eyes roamed from group to group, but didn't find anyone he could talk to. He felt like an outsider. He may have married into the family, but he'd never been accepted. Truth be told, he'd felt more like a part of the family before he married Sarah. As the driller on the oil field, he'd earned the respect and trust of not only Mr. Dillingham, but also each partner in the oil industry. That all changed the day he and Sarah eloped.

Sarah spotted him and waved him over. He took a deep breath and headed into the rattlesnake pit. His only relief came from Sarah, who always made him feel welcome and loved.

Mallory tracked Joe as he walked over to her sister and lovingly slid his arms around her waist. Her blue eyes narrowed as she watched him place a kiss on the back of Sarah's neck. Her head started hurting.

Pressure increased as she watched them talking and laughing. She hated how at ease Joseph always seemed around Sarah, like she was the center of his world or something. *Why hasn't he ever looked at me that way?* Mallory fumed. Being far prettier than Sarah, and more independent, it should have been a no brainer that Joseph fell for her. She knew how to run the oil business and worked side by side with the men on the field sites.

Yet, her little sister always managed to attract all the attention. Why was it that dowdy, little Sarah, who always depended on everyone else to take care of her, could wrap every man around her finger without trying? What did she have that made people go out of their way to protect her?

As an infant, she'd caused their mother's death. Mallory never understood why their mother had chosen to risk her life by giving birth instead of aborting. Hadn't her mother cared about her or Robert at all? And what about her husband? He'd been left trying to raise three kids and run the oil business by himself.

Her mother's protection of the unborn baby while ignoring the effects on the rest of the family, only served to fuel her hatred when the new baby finally came home. Her father's doting attitude didn't help. How could he love the little thing that had killed his wife?

As the years went by, the situation only got worse. It seemed that everyone, who met Sarah, fell in love with her. She smiled sweetly, said the right things, acted appropriately and obeyed the rules. Even Robert had developed a tender spot for his baby sister, a tenderness that he never shared with her. But that was all right, she didn't need someone taking care of her.

Mallory Dillingham stood on her own two feet. She never gave in to demands, but expected them to be obeyed when ordered. She didn't need love. Power made her heart sing, calling like a lover's whisper. She fought for what she wanted. Maybe Sarah got things by being weak and helpless, but she preferred to take her heart's desire.

Right now the object of her attention was Joseph Barnes. He'd swept onto the scene, working on the oil rigs and quickly advanced into the driller position because of his extensive knowledge and hard work. Of course, she'd pushed for the position, knowing that she'd get to spend more time with him. He'd been grateful to her but never moved the relationship beyond business.

Then, he'd met Sarah. They'd kept the relationship a secret for several months before coming out into the open, and a few months after that they eloped. It wasn't fair! She had known Joseph first and worked hard at getting him to notice her, and little Miss Sarah snatched him up in six months with her little, *help me I'm so defenseless that I need a big, strong man to protect me*, routine.

Well, the tide was turning. It may have taken her another three years, but she'd finally gotten her man. There's no way he'd stay with Sarah after last night. He may still be in shock, but once that wore off he'd come begging her to take him to bed again.

She smiled and sipped her Martini. She couldn't wait to see the look on precious little Sarah's face when she learned that her husband had fallen in love with her sister.

"Mallory, did you hear me?"

She shook the image from her mind and focused on the little toad of a man standing in front of her. "I'm sorry, William, I was lost in thought."

"I was saying that the quarterly figures suggest that Dillingham Oil is losing profits." She watched his pudgy face flap like a bulldog as he continued on and on about the finances of the company. She didn't need his long-winded explanation, she heard all she needed to know – the company was losing money.

Thankfully, she was saved from his blubbering by Sarah.

"Everyone, I'd like your attention for a moment." Her voice was soft and didn't carry over everyone's conversation, so Joe whistled, just about causing the drink glasses to shudder.

Everyone stopped talking and looked at him. Sarah's cheeks had two red spots on them. "I'm sorry," she hesitated, "but Joe and I have an announcement." Her eyes darted to Joe. He nodded to go on. "I had planned on waiting and talking with my family privately first. But, seeing as how our closest friends are here tonight, we've decided to share the news with everyone."

She stopped and took a deep breath.

Mallory noted that Sarah felt uncomfortable. *Could this be it?* She wondered. *Had Joe already decided to leave her?* She couldn't believe it was happening so fast. Her mind swam with joy.

"I found out a few months ago that I'm going to have a baby."

Joe smiled and Sarah patted her belly. "I'm just starting to show," she said, proudly.

The hush over the room was broken by Mallory's Martini glass shattering on the floor. The pressure from earlier squeezed her brain until her head felt like it might explode.

"Are you all right?" William asked.

"I'm fine." Mallory touched her head, hoping to alleviate the pain. She needed a pressure vent like the ones on the oil rigs.

"You look quite pale."

"I'm just in shock over the news of becoming an aunt." Her fake smile seemed to satisfy him.

Mallory wiped at her red suit. "Will you excuse me? I'm soaked, I need to go change."

"Of course." William headed to the group surrounding the new parents-to-be.

As Mallory headed toward the door she heard her father exclaim, "Praise be, I'm going to be a grandpa?" The round of hugs and congratulations grated on her nerves.

Even Joseph seemed to be accepted into the group on good terms, now that he'd produced an heir for Dillingham Oil. His smile beamed brighter than the sun at high noon. He shook hands with everyone and even earned a hug from Richard.

"Santiago," Mallory yelled. "Find Maria and have her clean up the broken glass before someone gets hurt."

"I'll do it right now," the maid offered.

"Did I say for you to do it?" Mallory snapped. "I want that lazy daughter of yours to start earning her pay."

"Right away, ma'am." The maid's wrinkled face tightened and her dark eyes narrowed. She curtsied and left.

Mallory stomped out into the hallway, mumbling under her breath. "Stupid, lazy, incompetent help."

She continued her tirade all the way up the stairs and into her room. When the door closed tightly, she let out a scream that rattled the windows. "I don't believe that traitor." She ripped her jacket open without unbuttoning it. "Just when I finally get my plan in motion, she has to go and ruin everything."

She managed to unzip the skirt, stepped out of it, and went to her closet. "I'm not letting anyone spoil my plans." She pulled out a blue, velvet dress. "There's more than one way to skin a snake."

The dress may have been long but the split went so far up that you could see her third vertebra. The V-neck plunged down so low that her breasts were hanging out. Mallory smiled at her reflection. "Every man in the room will be watching me, even Joseph." *Maybe little Miss Sarah was able to get impregnated by her husband, but I'm going to get him body and soul.* The determined look shining from her blue eyes made her smile even more. "We'll see who wins, little sister."

Mallory entered the parlor again, receiving the effect she wanted. Every man stopped his conversation and watched her walk across the room. The women gaped and whispered about the inappropriate attire. Words like; shameful, indecent, and humiliating were used by the gentler more respectable southern women, while the bolder ones used words like; hussy, slut and harlot.

But she didn't care what they said about her. They were jealous and always had been. Most of their husbands and sons lusted after her. Some had even slept with her. Who wouldn't want a piece of this action? *I'm hotter than Dillingham stock*, she thought as she weaved through the crowd.

Stopping by her sister she smiled. "Sarah, darling. I don't know what to say." She reached out and hugged her. "Congratulations."

"Thank you."

"Joseph. I can't believe it. You, a *dad*." She hugged Joe a little too tight, rubbing up against him so seductively that a few gasps were heard.

"Mallory, can we have a talk?" Richard grabbed her arm, leading her through the crowd. His face reddened as they entered the empty hallway. "What in blazes do you think you're doing?"

"Saying congratulations to my sister."

"You are causing trouble." Richard folded his arms across the width of his chest. "I won't stand for it. Whatever your problem is, you'd better get over it. I won't have you messing with your sister or causing a scene."

"I'm not." Mallory pouted. "I gave her and Joseph hug."

"What is this thing you're wearing?"

"My new dress."

"Go put something on that covers your body," he insisted. "And stay away from Joe."

"You're not the boss of me." Her rounded nose rose slightly.

"I'm your father and I'll not have you causing trouble because you're jealous."

"Who says I'm jealous?"

Richard stepped closer, his voice low. "You've been jealous since the day they married. It's time to let hurt feelings go and get on with your life. Let your sister and Joe live their lives peaceably."

"Why is everything about Sarah?" She stood nose to nose with her father. "I'm part of this family too."

"Then start acting like it."

"Why is it when I want something it's wrong? Why does Sarah get everything she wants?"

"You always want what you can't have." Richard's tone softened, "I don't understand you, Mallory. You have all the boys chasing after you, yet you ignore them."

"Because they're boys." She crossed her arms. "I want a man."

"You can't have your sister's husband, or any other woman's husband for that matter. It's time to grow up, Mallory. Stop parading around half naked like a hussy and act like a lady." With that he turned on his heel and left.

Mallory glared after him for a long time. "All right, Daddy." Her lips snarled. "If that's the way you want to play it." She stomped upstairs.

The smiles and sighs of relief were audible when Mallory reappeared more appropriately dressed in a black suit. Dinner progressed without another major eruption, but Mallory watched Sarah and Joseph closely.

Her sister was practically beaming with happiness and proud papa wasn't any better. The ladies were already talking about a baby shower and Richard seemed ecstatic to be a grandfather. Although why any man would be glad to be old enough to have grandchildren was beyond Mallory's comprehension. She didn't even want to be a mother, let alone a grandmother.

The idea of a baby rolled around her head. She'd worked too long and hard to let anyone or anything stand in her way, so what if a baby was on the way? Mallory wasn't about to alter her plan. The baby would still have its mother and the rest of the family. It's not like Joseph wouldn't be around, he just wouldn't be married to Sarah.

She smiled to herself, feeling satisfied that this new development wouldn't stop her scheme. Her conscience was clear.

Mallory joined the rest of the family for breakfast. "Where's Robert?" she asked.

"I haven't seen him." Richard replied.

"William and the shareholders are going to be here soon. I'd think he'd want to be here and know what's going on with the business." Mallory sat down across from Sarah.

"You know as well as I do that Robert's head is in politics, not business."

"Strange, seeing as he'll inherit the oil business." Her tone stung with bitterness. She had the head for business and loved running the oil fields, but her brother would take over simply because he was a man.

"Mallory, we've been over this before. Robert is the oldest."

"But he doesn't even want to run the company. He'll drive it into the ground after you die and I'll be left destitute."

"I believe you're exaggerating." Richard smiled, slightly. "Besides, I'm not ready to keel over any time soon."

"I just don't understand why I can't run the business. I know the oil business and I want to do it."

"Mallory, you will have an equal partnership with your brother. I'm not leaving you out of anything."

"How is Robert going to be able to run a company if he's elected senator or even governor?"

"You've jumped way ahead. He's only running for state representative. He may not like being in office."

"I doubt that. He's always loved politics. Even when he was a boy he'd stay up and watch the elections all night."

"True." Richard laughed at the memory. "He wasn't even old enough to vote yet."

"And you think he's going to get bored in office?"

"Maybe not, but he will take his family respons-ibilities seriously."

"I just don't see the need when I'm ready and more competent than he'll ever be."

"And, ever so humble." Richard sipped his coffee.

"I'm not hungry anymore." She pushed her plate away.

"Don't see how you could resist that dry toast?" Joe smiled.

"Shut up." Mallory stood. "I need some air." Another minute with her sexist father and the smug faced Joe, and she'd lose her mind completely. Besides she had an errand to run before the meeting.

Robert stood on the balcony, kissing a beautiful brunette. His fingers dug into the long, curly hair. "I love your hair," he whispered.

"I love your lips," she said.

He kissed her again, sighing against her neck. "You make me crazy, Maria."

"You must be crazy." She looked into his blue eyes. "You're taking a big risk, sneaking out here like this."

"I can't help it. I hate these stolen moments. Why must we sneak around?"

"You know the answer as much as I do." She glanced out over the green lawn. "It's too risky being out here. Someone could be hiding in the bushes."

"I don't think anyone is following me. I'm not a spy."

"But the paparazzi always follow you around. Your picture is in all the magazines. You are the biggest playboy in Texas." She turned away from him, trying to hide the hurt feelings.

"I'm not a playboy anymore." He pulled her back into his arms. "The captions aren't true." He kissed her, long and deep. "You are the only woman for me."

"I wish that were true." Her brown eyes filled with tears. "But we'll never be able to have a normal relationship. We'll always have to hide."

"Not always." He hugged her close, inhaling the scent of citrus shampoo. "After I'm elected into office we'll start dating like a normal couple."

"You really believe that, don't you?"

"Don't you?" He pulled back, searching her eyes.

She looked sad. "You can never date, let alone marry, a maid."

"You won't be a maid after I marry you. You'll be Maria Dillingham, wife of the state representative."

"And what about becoming congressman or senator?" She laid a gentle hand along his cheek. "Do you think people will vote for you if your wife isn't a lady of stature. I'm the bastard child of a maid. As much as I love you, I'd only end up hurting you."

"Don't you say that again!" He scolded, gently. "I'll not run for office if it means losing you."

"Politics are your life."

"You, Maria Santiago, are my life." He kissed the palm of her hand. "You'll see. When the time is right, we'll be together and the people will love you just as much as I do."

"I want to believe you."

"Then trust me."

"I do." Maria leaned in for his kiss.

"I have a plan. We'll have everything we want." He kissed the tip of her nose. "Just be patient."

"He's so predictable," Mallory muttered.

She leveled the camera and snapped another picture. The last piece of the puzzle was in place. She'd completed her plan even sooner than expected. Who knew that her brother would make it so easy for her?

Chapter 4

"William, I need your help if I'm going to pull this off." Mallory lit a cigarette.

"I don't know how I can help."

"You said that the company is losing money. I need to make the shareholders aware of this." She paced around the room, her heels clicking against the office floor.

"I said the company is losing *profits*. There's a difference." William watched her agitated movements. His heart lurched as she put the cigarette between her lips and inhaled. "The shareholders are aware of certain wells slowing their production. That's to be expected after twenty years of drilling."

"That's my point." She exhaled a long line of smoke. "I have new ideas for drilling that can bring the profits back up. There's offshore drilling and drilling in Alaska. If we tap into these resources we can make more money."

"But there's a big risk involved."

"Look at these projections." Mallory handed him a manila folder. "Just look these figures over and get back to me." She stamped out her cigarette.

William glanced at the numbers. "I need to go over these in depth. Can I have a few days?"

"Of course." Mallory smiled.

"It would help if you had some family members on your side. I don't think the board will vote in your favor strictly on numbers alone."

"William," she sidled closer to him, "you've been Dillingham Oil's accountant for twenty-five years, surely if you're on my side that will sway others to follow."

"I don't think my opinion is worth as much as the stockholders'." The spicy smell of her perfume played havoc on his emotions. She'd never stood this close before. She'd never smiled like that. What on earth was she doing?

"I'll get you what you need," she whispered, running her long nails through his thinning hair. "And you'll get me what I want."

"I'll ... I'll see what I can do," he stammered.

Mallory smiled triumphantly. William's round head had beads of perspiration forming where his hairline used to be. If she weren't careful he might have a heart attack. That thought didn't bother her, except she needed him to help her sway the board members. After she had control of the company he could keel over and she wouldn't even shed a tear.

"I knew I could count on you." For good measure, she leaned in, capturing his lips with her own.

Joe reached for the handle on his bedroom door, when it suddenly opened. The maid almost bumped into him.

"Oh, Mr. Barnes, I'm sorry."

"No problem, Maria."

"I was only leaving some clothes for ..." she looked down at the floor, "for you."

"Okay. I thought maybe my wife had decided to have you start cleaning our room."

"No, sir. No one's mentioned a change in routine to me."

"Since Sarah's new disposition, I'm going to make a new order. I don't want her cleaning our room. Can you do it?"

"I'll put it on the schedule, sir." Maria fidgeted from foot to foot then tucked a piece of loose hair behind her ear. "If you'll excuse me, sir, I have other chores to finish."

"Yes, of course." He watched the maid walk down the hall, wondering what was wrong with her. Usually she chatted and joked around with him. Why did she seem so nervous? And what was up with the *sir*?

Heaving a heavy sigh, he walked into the room and felt a smack as cold as ice. On the bed was a neatly folded jacket, pair of socks, underwear and the shoe he'd left in Mallory's room. "Damn."

He raced out of the room and down the hall. "Maria, wait."

She stopped, clearly startled by his yelling. "Yes, sir."

"Where did you find those clothes?"

"I'd rather not say." She looked scared – perhaps upset was a better word.

"Please don't say anything."

She looked up surprised by the tone of his voice. "It's not my place to say anything." After all she was only hired help. It didn't matter to her what went on in the house, except, she'd always liked Joe. Viewed him as a hero, he made her feel like a relationship would be possible with Robert. After all, he'd been an ordinary worker and married Sarah. Maybe there was hope after all.

"Does anyone else know?" He sounded desperate.

"The maid who cleanses Miss Dillingham's room brought them to me. I recognized the jacket and shoe." Her tone was tight.

"Please, believe me, I never meant for this to happen." His blond brows furrowed. "I don't even know how it happened." He ran a hand through his thick hair. "I only remember bits and pieces of the other night. I guess I had too much to drink and somehow ended up spending the night with Mallory." His voice softened. "Sarah can't find out. Not now." His brown eyes grew intense, boring into her eyes. "She's pregnant, Maria. I have to protect not only my wife but my baby too. Please don't say anything."

"As I said before it's not my ..."

"Don't give me that speech." Joe broke in. "I'm not speaking to you as an employee. I'm asking you as a friend."

"As a friend?" Her dark brows rose. "I don't think you want my opinion as a friend."

"I don't blame you for being angry. I'm disgusted with myself right now."

"I'm not angry," she said. "I'm disillusioned."

"So am I." His face was so hard it looked ready to break.

"I promise not to say anything, but only to protect Sarah and the baby." Maria crossed her arms. "As for you and Mallory, you can both burn in Hades."

Joe watched her small figure walk down the long hall. He couldn't blame her for hating him. He hated himself at the moment.

"Sarah, are you feeling all right?" Richard watched his daughter pick at her food. "You always play with food when something's wrong."

"I'm fine, Dad. Just feeling a little nauseated."

"Is something wrong?" Joe dropped his fork. "Is the baby okay?"

"Everything is fine." She cupped his face with her hand.

"For Pete sakes, she's feeling a little ill," Mallory fumed. "Why are you all on edge?"

"Because we're worried," Joe snapped. "Why don't you leave her alone?"

"What are you going to do when she's in labor?" Mallory asked. "Don't tell me you're going to be one of those fathers who pass out."

"What's it to you anyway?" Joe challenged. "It's none of your business what I do."

"Alright, you two," Richard interrupted, "this isn't the time to be arguing."

"Dad's right." Sarah stood. "I'm sorry to ruin dinner, but I don't feel like eating. I'm going to go lie down."

"I'll come with you." Joe stood.

"Oh please." Mallory rolled her eyes. "She's not in kindergarten, you don't have to hold her hand."

"Mallory has a point, honey. You finish your dinner."

"The only thing Mallory has is a jealous streak," Robert said.

"And exactly what am I jealous of?"

"That Sarah's going to have a baby."

"The absolute last thing I want in this world is to have a messy, smelly, screaming child."

"Will both of you knock it off," Richard snapped. "I swear you still act like little children yourself. I'd like to eat my dinner in peace without all this bickering."

"Sorry, Dad." Sarah walked over and gave him a peck on the cheek. "I didn't mean to cause such a stir."

"It's not your fault, princess." He patted her hand. "Go get some rest."

"Of course nothing is ever her fault," Mallory sneered after Sarah left.

"See that's what I'm talking about," Robert said. "Jealous."

"Oh, Pleeease!"

"I'm having trouble digesting my food." Joe stood. "I think I'll take a walk."

"Are you two happy, now?" Richard's gray eyebrows arched.

"I'm not jealous," Mallory insisted. "But I am wondering why she took so long to tell us she's pregnant. She almost five months along."

"That is your sister's business," Richard reprimanded. "I want you to leave her alone."

"Yes, sir!" Mallory saluted. "Whatever you say, sir."

"So mature," Robert whispered, just loud enough for her to hear.

"Shut up," she whispered back.

Mallory sat up in the bed and watched William getting dressed. She knew she should say something like, "That was terrific." Or, "You're such a great lover." But she wasn't that good of an actress.

It had taken all of her mental strength and physical will power to suffer through the ordeal of sex with the pudgy, inapt man. His feeble groping and slobbering made her sick. He didn't leave her with the same feeling that Joseph had.

Sex with Joseph had been everything she'd expected. When they'd finished, she'd wanted more. A lifetime of sex with that man wouldn't be near enough time to enjoy all the pleasures he produced. On the opposite side, a week with William would make any woman want to commit suicide.

The man was differently better with numbers than with women, which was probably why he'd never married. William stuffed his shirt into his pants then fumbled with his tie.

"Come here and let me help you with that." Mallory smiled, sweetly.

He sighed at the sound of her voice, and obediently walked over to the bed.

She knotted the tie, then pulled him close and gave him a kiss. "Why do you seem so nervous? Surly this isn't your first time having sex."

"No." He shook his head, sending his cheeks flapping. "It's just the whole experience with you." He sat down on the edge of the bed. "I don't understand what a desirable woman like you is doing with me."

"William, you don't give yourself enough credit." She took a cigarette from the stand and lit it. "Why wouldn't any woman want to be with you?" She took a puff of the cigarette.

"I'm not very good at relationships."

"You're intelligent, hardworking, trustworthy."

"You make me sound like a dog." His round face reddened.

"You didn't let me finish." A trail of smoke curled around her head. "You're also charming and very sexy." She found it much easier to lie without his fat hands and lips touching her body.

His green eyes searched her blue ones. "I think you're lying."

"Why would I do that?"

"So that I'll help you steal the company away from your father."

"To be honest, William, I don't need you for that. In a few days I'll have everything I need to that on my own."

"Then why are we in this hotel room?"

"Because we couldn't do this at my place." She leaned forward and kissed him hard. Pulling back she looked into his eyes and mustered enough acting lessons to give him a smoldering look. She pushed back the sheet to offer him a view of her perfect body. As much as she loathed another encounter with this man, she had to get his mind back on her and not the company.

One statement had been true; he was smart. She needed him more than she wanted to let on. If having sex again meant his mind would be muddled for a while longer, then she'd do it. Whatever it took! That had always been her motto.

She put the cigarette in the ashtray and slid down on the bed. William hurriedly undid his tie. After his shirt came off, he started kissing her neck. Mallory closed her eyes and swallowed the lump of vomit stuck in her throat.

Mallory waltzed into the headquarters of the Democratic office. "Where's Robert?"

"I believe he's in a meeting with Senator Manning." The secretary looked over the small, square, wire rims of her glasses. Her brown hair had been pulled into a tight bun and the gray suit, although efficient looking, was very unflattering. "Do you care to leave a message?"

"No, I'll wait."

"He'll be a while." She narrowed her eyes.

"No problem." Mallory smiled. She loved getting under people's skin. However, after forty minutes the waiting started to irritate her. She tossed the magazine on the table and walked back up to the secretary. "How much longer?"

"I have no idea." She never looked up from her typing. "I told you he'd be a while."

"What could a senator and a want-a-be politician have to talk about for so long?"

The secretary stiffened. "Mr. Dillingham is going to be our state representative and will then become our congressman."

"Well he's a pesky, no good, older brother to me."

"I'd think you'd be more supportive of your own family." She slid the glasses back up her long nose.

"I wouldn't even cast a vote for him." Mallory laughed.

The office door opened and an older gentleman with gray hair walked out with Robert. As if on cue, Mallory smiled brightly. "Senator Manning, it's so nice to see you again."

"Miss Dillingham, you're looking marvelous."

"Why thank you." She extended her hand. "And how many times must I tell you to call me Mallory."

"My apologies, Mallory." He kissed the back of her hand.

She giggled like a schoolgirl. "I do declare that I get tingly sensations all over whenever you do that."

"Shall I stop?" He raised one gray brow. "Because it's the only pleasure I've had today."

"Not on your life." She leaned closer, whispering, "As long as your wife doesn't mind."

"No reason she should object to a simple kiss on the hand."

"The kiss on the hand isn't what I'm talking about." She walked with him to the door. "If you'd like to continue kissing elsewhere, you know the room number." She straightened and started laughing as if he'd just told a joke. "You are positively wicked, Senator Manning."

They played their parts well, but the secretary watched as the senator left and Mallory made her way back to the desk.

"Well, brother, dear, what did you and the senator talk about for so long?"

"Just preparing for the upcoming election." Robert seemed oblivious to the affair going on between Senator Manning and his sister. "He's giving me his support."

"How nice."

Robert walked back to his office, unaware of the glare his secretary gave his sister. "Is there something you need?" he asked over his shoulder.

"I need to speak to you about an urgent matter." She walked by the secretary, leaned over and whispered, "I wouldn't vote for Senator Manning either."

"Only sleep with him," she snorted before she could stop the words.

"Exactly why I wouldn't vote for him, he's not trustworthy." Mallory walked into the small office. "I think you need a decorator."

"I have what I need. Besides, this office is, hope-fully, temporary."

"Your office at Dillingham Oil is bigger than this."

"I don't care about the size of my office." He sat in his chair. "What's on your mind? You only visit when you want something."

"I'd like to play coy and say that's not true, but, it is." She shrugged her shoulders. "So, I'll get right to the point." She walked to the window. "I want your share of Dillingham stock."

"What?" He shot up. "You're out of your mind."

"You don't even care about the company."

"But I'm the next Dillingham to inherit it. I'd never let Dad down."

"How are you going to run the state of Texas and the oil company at the same time?"

"I'll have you to help me run the business. It's not like you don't have a say in the business. You hold twelve percent of the stock, same as me."

"But Father doesn't listen to any of my ideas."

"You need to take that up with him, not with me." He sat back down. "Now, I have a campaign to run."

"One you'll lose if you don't play your cards right."

"How can I play the wrong hand when I have you as a sister?" He smiled, tightly. "If you keep sleeping with all the senators, I'm a shoe in for governor."

"So you aren't dim-witted about my affairs after all." She walked back to the desk. "Just trying to help you out."

"The only person you ever try to help is yourself. I wouldn't be surprised to find out you had sex with Manning to persuade him *not* to support me."

"Dear, brother, do you really have so little faith in me?"

"Yes."

"That's fine treatment after I've come here to help you."

"And what can you help me with?"

"Your campaign, of course." She sat down.

"I think you've gone above the call of duty in that area."

"Not as far as I can go." Mallory pulled out a white envelope from her purse and tossed it on the desk.

Robert took the envelope, his blue eyes full of suspicion. Mallory had that determined look, which meant she wouldn't stop until she got what she wanted. He carefully pulled out the contents.

The glossy photos made his heart stop for a few beats. "Where'd you get these?" His voice was barely above a whisper.

"I took them." Mallory sat back in the chair, casually crossing her legs. "Why do you look so white? It's wonderful to see you in love."

"Mallory, don't play your stupid games with me." He leafed through a few more photos. Images of him kissing and embracing Maria jumped out at him. He became more agitated as he looked through the stack. Each set of prints was from different times. Although Maria had the same black uniform in each picture, her curly hair was in different styles. His clothes were all different.

"What'd you do, follow me around with a camera?" He glared at her. "There's at least a month's worth of shots here."

"Six weeks, to be precise." She smiled, innocently.

"How dare you!" He threw the pictures down on the desk. "I have a right to privacy in my own home."

"Why are you getting mad at me?" She leaned forward. "You're the one hiding your affair. Why don't you bring Maria out into the open? It seems to me if you love her, you'd want the world to know."

"My reasons are none of your business."

"Keep looking through the pictures. You haven't come to my favorite ones."

"I'm not playing your game, Mallory. Take your pictures and get out."

"I don't think your voters would approve of their state representative having a relationship with a maid."

"I don't believe the people will care." He put both hands on the desk and leaned closer. "She is an ordinary worker, just like most of my voters."

"Then why are you keeping it such a secret?"

"My personal life is none of your concern. Now get out before I do or say something you'll regret."

"You really shouldn't growl through your teeth like that. It makes you look like a dog."

"Mallory, get out," he shouted.

"I'm not done yet." She reached across the desk and with her long manicured nail moved some pictures to the side. "There they are." She smiled at him.

He looked down and his face went ashen.

"Not only are you hiding your relationship with our little maid, you literally are keeping her in the closet." Mallory sat back. "Even if the voters were willing to accept this sordid affair with Maria, I don't think they'd like the idea of the man representing them having sex in a cleaning closet."

"How did you get those? There's no way you were in there."

"Don't be disgusting." She frowned. "It was bad enough having to look at you two go at it like dogs in heat. I couldn't stomach being there."

"Damn it, Mallory." He rounded the desk and grabbed her by the shoulders. "Why are you doing this?"

She looked unruffled. "I want your shares of Dillingham Oil."

"What have you got scheming in that head of yours? Why are my shares so important to you?"

"I want control of the company."

His eyes narrowed. "You'd steal the company away from your own father?"

"Save the schoolboy speech." She brushed his hands aside and stood. "I merely want to implement my ideas and he's blocked me at every turn."

"And you think I'll help you?" He crossed his arms.

"If you don't I'm going to give these pictures to the tabloids." He looked out the window. "I think it would sabotage your chances of winning the election. Probably even ruin all chances of you ever getting any further in politics."

He ran a hand through his short, dark hair. "You're forgetting one thing. I've been in the tabloid lots of times, besides I'm not married."

"These pictures are too racy, even for a single candidate. No one is going to look at you the same way after seeing these. And, Maria will most definitely lose her job." Mallory crossed her arms. "This coming out now will ruin your whole plan of marrying her discreetly and slowing introducing her to the public as an acceptable wife."

"I could kill you." He flew across the room.

"Calm down, Robert." She ducked out of his way. "It's not that hard of a decision."

"You're asking me to pick between the woman I love and my father."

"I'm giving you the chance to back out of a company you don't want to run so you can focus on politics, which is the love of your life." She shrugged. "I'm doing you a favor, really."

"I hope you burn in hell."

"My eternal destination isn't the matter, at the moment." Walking over to the desk, she picked up the pictures. "You have twelve hours to decide then I'll release these to the press." Tossing the photos down, she left.

Chapter 5

Joe sat in the leather chair, flipping through the channels on the television set. He stopped at a Die Hard movie. He'd seen it a dozen times, but nothing else was worth watching.

He tried not to be disappointed that Sarah had backed out of watching a movie with him. Friday nights had been their designated movie night. However, she wasn't feeling well again. He wanted to suggest an abortion, but knew it was futile. Not only was Sarah determined to have the baby, he wanted it just as much.

But he worried something would go wrong. He'd had a funny feeling in the pit of his stomach ever since she told him the news. Was this a normal feeling? Why did he feel like he needed to protect both her and the baby? Maybe his feelings came from the guilt he felt, wanting to protect Sarah because he'd betrayed her.

He thought about seeing a shrink, but thought he was man enough to handle this on his own. Besides, he didn't want strangers knowing his personal business. Talking to Sarah was what he needed the most, and yet, that was the only thing he couldn't do. He wanted to tell her the truth and beg for forgiveness, but couldn't risk it.

"Is this where the party's at?" Mallory plopped down on the sofa. "What are you drinking?"

"Root beer."

"Wow, you party hard." She grabbed a handful of popcorn from the dish on the coffee table. "What's on?"

"Die Hard with a Vengeance."

"That's a rerun. Let's watch something else."

"I'm waiting for Sarah." He hated lying, however being alone with Mallory seemed inappropriate now.

"So, I'm not allowed to crash this party?" She crunched some popcorn.

"It's *our* movie night." His brown eyes were sharp and assessing.

"I have it on good authority that little Miss Sarah is sick." Mallory sighed. "If you ask me, she's doing a poor job of taking care of you."

"Sarah takes care of me just fine." His fingers tightened on the brown bottle.

"She can't even watch a movie with you." A fire glowed in the depths of her blue eyes. "I, on the other hand, know how to treat a man."

"The only person you know how to take care of is yourself."

"That's not true." She stood, and with the slow assurance of a spider, crept toward his chair. "I had you screaming and begging for more." She leaned over him, staring down into his dark, cold eyes. "And you had me doing the same." She straddled him. "We can have it again."

"I'm not drunk or stupid enough to fall into that trap again." He dumped her on the floor, then stood and walked a few steps away.

Mallory stood, indignantly brushing herself off. "You were much more fun drunk."

"You stay away from me and my wife or, I swear, I'll kill you." He stormed out of the room and down the hall.

She stared after him, her eyes blazing like blue coals, both fists bunched at her sides. She wanted him so much tonight. Needed him. After the lousy roll with William, she wanted someone who knew how to handle her. Not even Senator Manning seemed worth the effort. No man compared with Joseph.

A few tears slid down her cheeks. She brushed them away with the back of her hand, anger built up, rolling and rumbling. He had no business threatening her like that. She'd only offered him some pleasure. She couldn't believe he'd been fool enough to refuse. No man has ever ignored her.

Surely he wasn't in love with Sarah. He'd probably only married her to gain access to the family wealth. What was wrong with the two of them sharing some passion while he acquired his wealth? Well, he'd messed with the wrong Dillingham. No way she would let him go so easily. "You will be mine, Joseph Barnes."

Joe sat on the edge of the bed while Sarah kneaded his shoulders. "You have a huge knot." She applied more pressure. "How'd work go today?"

"We had another leak."

"You know what that does to the environment," she scolded, softly.

"Honey, I don't want you getting upset."

"I still have to protect the Earth. Our child isn't going to have a place to grow up if we don't start taking care of this land."

"Our child won't have a home if we can't drill for oil. That's what pays the bills."

"I'm not saying you can't drill, but you need to be more careful." She was always at odds with her family over this issue. They could never understand her need to protect the environment over profits. "Global warming is a big issue."

"I know, honey, but we take all the precautions we can." He reached back and captured her hand. Bringing it to his mouth, he placed a kiss on it. "I should be pampering you." He turned to face her.

"Why? I haven't worked on the rig all day." She didn't want to let the subject drop so easily, but she also didn't want to fight.

"You're carrying my child."

"I'm carrying our child." Sarah smiled. "And it's not hard." She playfully swatted his bare shoulder. "Turn around and let me work that kink out."

Joe obeyed, grateful for a wife who'd rub him down every night. "Your fingers are magic," he sighed. *This is much better than watching a movie*, he thought. After a few minutes Sarah said, "Why don't you take your jeans off and lie down? I'll rub your back."

He sprawled on the bed in nothing but his underwear. "This feels like heaven."

Sarah leaned down, kissing his neck and spreading across his shoulders. "I love the feel of your muscles." As her hands kneaded his muscles, her lips tasted his skin.

Joe tensed. Rolling over he looked into her warm, hazel eyes. "Is it okay?"

She smiled. "There's no reason we can't make love."

"But you haven't been feeling well."

"I know it's been a long time, but it had nothing to do with the pregnancy." She seated herself next to him. "When I found out I was pregnant, I was scared. My sex drive diminished because of mental issues, not physical ones." She tenderly cupped his face. "I feel ready now."

"Are you sure?" His body was already hard. He loved the way she made him feel, but didn't want to risk the baby.

"Yes." She bent over, capturing his lips. "I love you, Joe." She slid down next to him.

"I love you too." He rolled on top of her. After carefully removing her clothes, he noticed the swell of her stomach. Bending over and placing kisses on it, he said, "I love you too, little one."

As they made love, his only thought centered on protecting them both.

Having more energy the next few days, Sarah joined the family for both breakfast and dinner. No one could deny the extra step in her walk, and her face glowed like the sun.

Mallory watched as Sarah devoured two full plates. "How huge do you want to get?"

"I am eating for two." Sarah smiled, sweetly.

"You'll still have to lose the weight after the baby is born." Mallory sipped her coffee.

"I don't care about her weight," Joe said.

"You will when she looks like a hog."

"That's enough, Mallory," Richard reprimanded. "You've done nothing but make obscene remarks ever since Sarah announced the pregnancy. I want you to stop."

Mallory snarled and bit into her toast.

"It's all right, Dad." Sarah's calm attitude seemed to settle everyone. "Mallory is entitled to her own opinion."

"I don't need you defending me." She hated when Sarah did that, especially when she purposely tried upsetting her. "I'm a big girl and can take care of myself."

"Well, then, I'd appreciate you staying away from my husband." Sarah smiled, tensely. "Trying to steal my husband isn't going to make your life any better."

"For Pete sakes, what would I want with your life?" Mallory growled. "You are a pathetic nobody who leans on everybody else for protection. I prefer to stand on my own two feet."

"You don't stand on your own feet," Robert interjected. "You walk over everybody. You stand on the dead souls you create." He threw his napkin down and stood. "Someday it's going to catch up to you." He stormed out.

"What soured his milk this morning?" Mallory asked.

Sarah looked to Joe, then to Mallory. "Stay away from my family." Her tone was dangerous. "I'll do whatever I need to protect them."

"That's some threat coming from little Miss Betty Homemaker." Mallory laughed, although Sarah had never looked so serious before.

"Shut up," Joe said.

"Make me."

He clenched his teeth so tight that his jaw hurt, but he didn't dare say another word. The wicked gleam in Mallory's eyes threatened his world.

"Now, if you're all done picking on me this morning, I have work." She wiped her mouth, tossing the linen napkin on her plate and stood.

"Quit acting like you're hurt and innocent." Sarah stood too, meeting Mallory's eyes. "You leave a path of destruction wider than an exploding star, and act as though you've done nothing wrong. You sure can play the injured animal routine when it suits your needs."

"That's your area of expertise, not mine." Mallory placed her hands on the table and leaned forward, staring her sister in the eyes. "Are you mad because you think I'm stepping on your territory?"

"The only territory I'm protecting is my family. I won't tell you again, stay away from my husband."

"I don't recall that marriage means owning anyone. Joe is a big boy and can decide for himself who he wants."

"Stop it!" Richard stood. "Mallory, go to work. Sarah, go rest." He looked at Joe. "You be the referee for a while. I'm going to the office." He left.

Joe stood, slipping his arm around Sarah's waist. "Come on, honey. I'm going to tuck you into bed before I leave for work."

"I'm not tired."

"Then watch some TV, or read for a while, but you have stressed yourself out and I want you to promise to stay in bed today."

"That's not necessary." She smiled. "I'm fine."

"But I'll be worried about you all day if I don't know you're in good hands."

"For Pete sakes," Mallory grumbled. "My breakfast is going to come back up if I listen to you two any longer." She stomped out.

Joe called Maria, instructing her to keep Sarah in bed, or call him if Sarah wouldn't listen. With those orders, he kissed his wife on the nose and left for the field.

Mallory tapped her pen against the table as her father droned on about why they couldn't afford a new oil rig. "Eight hundred thousand dollars is a lot of money when our old ones work fine."

"But we have the cost of repairing them," Mallory said. "Not to mention, this rig is computerized, it will show us where the oil is in the ground. How much money is wasted when we drill for weeks or months and hit nothing? Don't you see, how this machine will eliminate all the guesswork?"

"Mallory, there will always be guesswork , it's part of the oil business." The shareholder with gray hair, slipped off his glasses. "You can't have one hundred percent guarantees, even with new equipment."

"Well, no, not a hundred percent, but it's a closer percentage than the old rigs."

"It's not cost effective," Richard said.

"You're only saying that because it's my idea. You shoot down every idea I come up with, and you get your friends, here, to back you up."

"These are the shareholders in the company. I'm saying no because they don't want to invest. If they thought it's a good idea then I'd reconsider." Richard leaned back in his chair. "Why don't we take vote?"

"Like that would help," Mallory whispered under her breath. Some of these men had been with the company since they were babies bouncing on their grandfather's knee. Their fathers sat on the board and their grandfathers were shareholders from the time her grandfather had started the company. Others were new, but seemed afraid to go against the majority.

"All in favor of buying a new oil rig raise your hand," Richard said.

Mallory sighed, but raised her hand, even though she knew she'd be the only one. To her surprise, two other men raised their hands. Robert did also, although he didn't look happy about it.

"Four in favor," Richard continued. "All opposed." The rest of the hands went up. "Ten against. The motion fails."

Maybe she'd failed today, but there was a silver lining. Two other members had been on her side. If she worked on them, maybe she could sway their votes. Perhaps, there were even others who'd just not had the guts to stand up to her father. She had a lot of work to do.

"Who wants to make a motion to adjourn the meeting?" Richard ended the meeting then said goodbye to the others. When the room emptied, he walked over to Mallory and sat next to her.

"I'm sorry your feelings got hurt."

"My feelings aren't hurt." She smiled. "And, you're not sorry, so quit lying."

"Mallory, why are you so distant?"

She arched a dark brow. "Why do you care?"

"You're my daughter." He sounded hurt. "I love you."

"You love Sarah, just like everyone else."

"I don't understand this competition you've created with your sister. Why does everyone have to be on sides?"

"The world creates the lines. I simply chose the side I want."

"What about family? What side are we on?"

"That, my dear father, is up to you." She stood, walking to the door. "If I were you, I'd hurry and choose. Time is running out." She opened the door and left.

Joe blew on his hands, pulled his gloves on, and set his hard hat on top of his head. The forty-five degree weather made his joints stiffen. He didn't think he should feel so stiff at thirty-four years old, but the oil field had a way of aging your body well beyond its years.

The catcalls and whistles from the crew drew his attention to a female walking towards the rig. Even clad in blue jeans and a flannel shirt, there was no mistaking the sway of her hips and the dark hair under the yellow hard hat. Mallory Dillingham, another element that aged a person's body.

He took the metal steps down to the lower deck. "What are you doing here?" He asked as he reached the landing.

"Don't take that tone with me," she insisted. "I've come to check on the progress of the rig."

"I don't need the boss's daughter hanging around this place. It's not safe."

"I'll take this opportunity to remind you that I own and run the business. I'm not just the boss's daughter. And, I know far more about running an oil rig than the average woman." Her eyes bore into him. "May I remind you that you were a simple roughneck before I promoted you to driller."

"Your father promoted me because of my experience."

"You're awful young to be commanding an oil rig." Mallory pointed to her chest. "I recommended you. I pulled strings to get you this position. You owe me big time, Joseph Barnes."

"I made driller because of my experience and hard work. I command this rig because the crew respects me. You can twist the facts all you want, but you can't scare me, Mallory. I made it here on my own skills and your father will confirm that."

"I put you in this position and I can take you down."

"Think what you like. I don't have time to stand here debating with you." Joe turned toward the steps.

"You owe me, Joseph." Mallory walked up behind him, so close she could smell the salt from his body mixing with the dirt, and oil from the land. "You owe me."

Joe turned around and found her body so close, he nearly brushed her breasts. "I believe I paid you a few weeks ago."

"The debt isn't paid in full."

"It's all you're going to get. Stay away from me and my wife."

"You shouldn't threaten me like that, especially since I came out here to help you."

"You can't help me, and I don't want anything you offer."

"You know, this is a very dangerous job. You can lose a thumb or even a hand by throwing that chain. You could be crushed by a fifty ton pipe. Or, you can be fired for making a mistake." She tilted her head back, staring him down. "I can get you a cushy office position. You could even become a board member. Just think of it, sitting around in an air-conditioned office, making plans and talking strategies with my father. Choosing and firing the workers. Learning how to make money and spending it as fast as it comes." Her red lips were inches from his. "I can make all of that happen and more. If only you'd trust me."

Joe grabbed her shoulders and pushed her away. "I have all I want with Sarah."

"You're a stupid fool," she spat. "My sister can't give you anything."

"She gives me love, Mallory. Something you'll never understand."

"What about the job?"

"I like what I do." He tipped his hard hat back. "Now if you'll excuse me, my crew needs my guidance." He disappeared up the steps.

"We'll see about that." Mallory stomped up the stairs and demanded that he show her the figures for the drill site.

Mallory brushed her hair behind her ears then placed the silver brush on the vanity. It had been two weeks since she'd visited the work site, and four weeks since Joseph had made love to her. She couldn't wait any longer. Wanting him filled her days and consumed her nights. Hopefully, the note she sent with her maid would make him come to her.

Just as the thought formed in her mind, a knock boomed on her door. She jumped, then, smiled. He'd come to her. One more time.

"Come in." She played coy.

The door opened with a thud. "What in the blazes do you think you're doing?" He held up the note. "Don't you ever threaten me!" He crumbled it up and threw it on the floor. "I'm no servant to be summoned at your disposal."

"Oh, Joseph, I don't think of you as a servant." She stood, her sheer, white gown, floating to the floor. "I believe you are so much more." Her husky voice filled the room, which seemed to shrink in size as she walked closer. "You're my lover," she barely whispered the words. "That's a big difference."

"Stop it." Joe pushed her back a few steps. "Whatever you think is going to happen, isn't. Get that through your thick skull."

She stepped closer, wrapping her arms around his waist. "I've never been one to take no for an answer." She brushed against him.

Joe grabbed her wrists. "You're going to take it now." He pushed her away. "I'm not drunk enough to fall into bed with you."

"I wouldn't be so sure." She smiled, her red lips emitting doom.

"Stay away from me, and Sarah."

"I hear poor Sarah isn't feeling well." Mallory pouted.

"Her blood pressure is a little high, that's all."

"Really? I heard she has to be on bed rest as much as possible." A red painted nail tapped the corner of her mouth. "I wonder how finding out that her husband cheated on her will affect the baby?"

"Mallory, what do you want from me?"

"I think I've made myself perfectly clear on that." She stepped closer.

"And I've made myself clear." He put his hands on her shoulders, halting her progress. "It will never happen again."

Mallory laughed. "We'll see." She walked over to the closet, opened the door and put a DVD in the player.

Joe stood, horrified, as images of him and Mallory appeared on the screen. She'd just tossed him a package and he ripped it open with his teeth. "I'll put them on and take them off." The words made him feel weak. The images made him want to vomit.

Mallory smiled at his reaction. "I have the whole night on tape. We can watch every moment and relive it." She stepped closer, carefully judging his mood. He seemed mad enough to strangle her. "Perhaps Sarah would enjoy it."

"Stop it." Joe yelled, tears filling his eyes. "Why are you doing this?"

"I want you, Joseph. And, I always get what I want." She brushed up against him. "That was the best night of my life. We can have it again."

Joe stood, transfixed, watching the screen. What had gotten into him that night? He'd drunk too much before and never wound up making such a mistake. "I can't do that again."

"Oh, yes you can." She kissed his neck. "Or, I'll have to show this to Sarah."

"No." Tears streamed down his face. "It'll destroy her."

Mallory brushed her chest up against him like a dog in heat. "Then make love to me again."

"No."

"Yes." She kissed his lips. "I want to feel your hands all over my body." She took his hands, brushing them across her chest.

Joe watched as her nipples hardened beneath the thin material. He could feel the heat from her body. He hated how his body reacted to her.

"Kiss me, Joseph." Her husky voice floated around him, drowning him in sorrow. "Touch me." She squeezed his hands around her nearly naked breasts. "Make love to me." She captured his lips with hers. "I'm yours to do with as you please."

"That could be dangerous." He pictured his hands strangling her thin, white neck.

"Anger can hold just as much passion as love." She kissed him, sealing his fate.

Chapter 6

Joe crawled into bed, cuddling next to Sarah, careful not to wake her as she needed her rest. He'd talked to the doctor and found out that her blood pressure had shot up and her protein levels were high. From now on she had to watch her diet, exercise and reduce stress. She also needed as much bed rest as possible.

He inhaled the sweet scent of flowers and felt his body relax. In the darkness of the night he could pretend everything was normal. He could forget all about Mallory and his betrayal. He could be the faithful, loyal husband he wanted to be.

As the night unfolded, he dreamed about the family they'd created. He pictured his little girl twirling around in circles in a ballet skirt. He heard her sweet voice saying, "Daddy, I love you." He watched as Sarah helped her bake cookies, and gave their daughter a bath. They'd both tuck her in bed every night and no child would be more loved. They'd have the perfect family.

Then, dawn would come, and his dreams would be pushed aside as cold, hard reality crashed around him. Another day of pretending, lying, and avoiding Mallory made him cringe. How had his life become so complicated?

"Are you getting up?" Sarah leaned over and kissed him, softly.

"In a minute." He played with her wispy bangs.

"You used to jump up in the mornings, now I have to drag you out of bed." Her loving eyes showed signs of concern. "Are you feeling well?"

"I'm fine." He kissed the tip of her nose. "I just want to spend more time with you."

"Joe, I hope you know you can tell me anything. I'm not as delicate as you think."

"Yes, you are." His heart ached. Coming clean and throwing himself on her mercy was the only way to beat Mallory at her own game. However, he knew it would destroy his marriage. He could never risk that.

"I want to help."

"There's nothing to help with. You concentrate on the baby and I'll take care of the rest."

"We're supposed to be partners," she sighed.

"We are." Joe went into the bathroom. "What's bringing this on?"

"I can't help but feel like you're hiding something."

"I promise you, I'm not." His hands were tied. Lying seemed the only way to protect her and the baby.

"I've got him." Mallory smiled, laying the letter on her desk.

"Got who?" William looked puzzled.

"John Colthrop agrees with the letter we sent out." She walked around to the front of her desk, where William sat and hugged his head to her breasts. "That must have been one hell of a letter you wrote."

"It...it wasn't much." Beads of perspiration formed on his forehead. "I just informed him of the value of new technology and the soundness of your ideas to move the company into this century."

"I like that." She smiled seductively. "You make me sound so smart." She bent her head and kissed him.

"You didn't need me for that." His breath came in short gasps. "You are smart and beautiful."

"William, you give me too much credit." She swallowed the distaste from the last kiss and forced her lips to pucker once again. "I could never have accomplished this without you."

"My letters only gained the votes of the two younger members on the board. They are more than happy to accept change. Being young makes them part of a different world, one that your father and older members are afraid of. So, they weren't too hard to convince." He pulled Mallory down into his lap. "Justin Walker, however, has been your father's biggest supporter. They grew up together. How you ever managed to get his support is beyond my comprehension." He kissed her neck.

"Leverage, my dear, William."

"You didn't sleep with him, did you?" His body stiffened.

"Don't be ridiculous." She laughed. "However, the fact that I had pictures of him with a young brunette did help convince him." She ran her hand through his thinning hair. "I don't have to be the one having all the sex to get what I want."

"That's how you got me."

"You are an entirely different story." She kissed him with as much passion as she could muster.

"You still have a problem," William said breathlessly. "You only have four other members on your side. That's five total with your vote. You need one more to take over the company."

Mallory stood, pacing a few steps away. "Why do you have to always rain on my parade?" She walked to the window and looked out over the city of Huston. "I'm working on my sister. If I get her on my side, I'll have all the votes I need to take over the company."

"Sarah is very loyal to your father."

"I said I'm working on it."

Robert held Maria as she cried into the crook of his neck. "Why is she doing this to us?"

"I don't know," he sighed. But he did know. Mallory wanted his help in taking over the oil company that his father had worked a lifetime building. Money. Greed. Power. Those were the only things that mattered to his sister.

"Why can't she just leave us alone?"

"She's using our relationship to further her ambitions," Robert said. "I wish I could change things but I can't."

Maria punched his chest. "You jerk," she cried. "You're supposed to say that our love is worth fighting for. Why are you rolling over and letting her get away with destroying us?"

"I'm not rolling over," he defended. "I'm trying to be diplomatic and save both our relationship and my political career."

"Quit being so sensible." Maria wiped her tears away. "You're too cute when you do that."

He smiled for the first time in weeks. "I'd like to quit, but it's part of being a politician."

Maria finally smiled. "I hate when you're so diplomatic. It makes it hard to be mad at you."

"I don't understand why you're mad at me. I didn't do anything."

"Exactly. You're not fighting for us. I'm tired of sneaking around and now we have incriminating pictures hanging over our heads."

"I didn't take them."

"But you're siding with her. That gives her power over us."

"I can't change things." He paced back and forth. "Don't you think I'd give everything, including my life, to get out from under this? I feel like a rattler trapped in a cage. I have no choice but to give in to her demands."

"And risk losing me?" Tears brimmed in her brown eyes again.

"I don't want that." He reached out, embracing her. "I will think of something, just give me time."

"How long do you expect me to wait?" She looked up into his blue eyes. "I've been waiting for years and the time has never been right to introduce me to your family, let alone to your voters. I'm tired of hiding, Robert. I'm tired of being the well-kept secret of the future representative of Texas." She pulled out of his embrace. "I need to know that I matter more than your campaign."

"You do," he said.

"I need more than words, Robert. I need proof."

"What do you want me to do?" He threw his hands up in the air. "Do you want me drop out of the race? Give up my political aspirations? Do you want me to marry you?" He stormed around the room. "What exactly do you want?"

"I want all of the above." Her voice was so low he could barely hear her words. "I want you to love me." With tears streaming down her cheeks, she left him to his thoughts.

Mallory looked over the data for the new site. "This looks good."

"Both the gravity meter and the magnetometer show oil flow activity." The geologist smiled. "Even the sniffers have detected the smell of hydrocarbons."

"Very good." Mallory looked up. "What about the seismology readings?"

"The Thumper trucks will be arriving later today," he explained. "And the seismologists will be looking for signs of oil and gas traps, in the following week."

"Well, the surface rocks, terrain and satellite images look promising," she smiled. "Good work."

"Miss Dillingham, you do realize that even with the best equipment there is only a ten percent success rate."

"I know." She handed him the clipboard. "But my gut feeling has never let me down."

"All right, ma'am." He took the clipboard and headed toward his crew.

Joe approached. "What are you doing here?"

Mallory's blue eyes narrowed. "Don't take that tone with me." She stepped closer. "I'm the boss."

"You're the boss's daughter." Joe hid his smile as her body stiffened.

"I'd watch your tongue, if I were you."

"Well, now, thankfully you're not me."

Mallory stepped closer, her boot crunching the hard, dry ground. "I'm going to be in control someday, Joseph Barnes, and you'd best be on my good side when that happens."

"You have no good side," Joe sneered down at her. He grabbed her wrist as her hand flew toward his face.

"I'll make you pay for that remark," she threatened.

"You already have." His hand tightened around her wrist.

"I don't understand why you can't relax and enjoy our time together?" She pulled her hand away, rubbing the red mark he left. "I enjoy every minute of it." Her voice turned soft, sultry.

"I hate every second." Joe's brown eyes hardened. "I'll never come to you willingly."

"I don't care whether you're willing or not." She brushed against his chest. "As long as you come."

"I hate you." The venom in each word was stronger than the poison of rattlers.

"And, I love the way you make my body sing." She smiled. "It's been a while, are you meeting me tonight?"

"No."

"It's not a question, Joseph." Her blue eyes snapped. "Meet me at nine."

"No."

"Then poor, little Sarah will see the video of us." She stepped back. "You don't want that do you?" Turning, she walked away.

Joe took his hard hat off and wiped the sweat off his forehead. How had his life gotten so entangled with a witch like her?

Joe waited until Sarah's breathing became slow and steady before he snuck out of the bedroom. He hated this sneaking around. Hated being with Mallory. But, he didn't know what to do. Sarah would never forgive him, and he'd not only lose her love, he'd lose his unborn child too. No way could he risk that, and yet he couldn't continue with Mallory. There had to be a way out. He wouldn't rest until he found it.

"You're late," Mallory fumed.

"I had to wait until Sarah fell asleep." He closed the door behind him.

"That better be the truth." The idea of him and Sarah together sickened her.

"What do you know about truth?"

"As much as you do." She smiled, sauntering toward him. "Relax, Joseph." She rubbed her hands over his chest. "I'll take good care of you." Her hands slipped inside his robe, rubbing his bare chest.

"Sarah takes good care me." He smiled as the barb hit its mark.

"Shut up about Sarah." She stalked over to the table against the wall. "Do you want a drink?" She held up a crystal container of scotch.

"No."

"Oh, c'mon, it'll loosen you up." She poured some scotch in a glass and walked back over to him. "You need to loosen up." She pressed the drink in his hand.

"Drinking is what landed me here in the first place." He shoved the drink away.

"You never give up, do you?" She downed the amber liquid in one swallow.

"Do you?"

"Never." She walked over to the closet and opened the door. "Shall we watch a video?" She held up the DVD. "I just love a good romance."

"There is no romance when you're involved."

"Why are you so cynical?"

"It's not cynicism. It's hatred," he clarified.

Mallory smiled, undoing her robe and letting it pool around her feet in a satin puddle. Her red satin teddy barely covered her curves. She walked closer. "I don't care what it is, as long as it turns you on." She reached up, grabbed his head and brought his lips close to hers. She kissed him so hard she drew blood.

"Stop." He drew away.

"Maybe we won't need the video after all." Her red lips formed a seductive smile. "You like what I have to offer, you just won't admit it."

"I love my wife and child," he said.

"I'm not talking about love." She crossed the room. "I'm talking about sex."

"It's the same thing," he insisted.

She shook her head, sending the dark tresses bouncing over her creamy, white shoulders. "It's not the same thing, and you know it."

"Why are you doing this, Mallory?" He was tired of her game.

"Because I like how you make me feel." She walked back, standing in front of him, the drink in her hand, tempting him, slightly. "I always get what I want."

"Even at the expense of other people's feelings?"

"I don't care about anyone else." She took a long, slow drink.

"That's the difference between you and Sarah."

"Exactly." She brushed up against him. "And, you love it."

"I love Sarah." He stepped back.

"Stop pretending, we're alone." She brushed up against him, once more.

"You're probably videotaping this, too."

"Nonsense. I only needed one tape." She took another sip. "Do you want to watch it?"

"I want to stop this charade."

"Well," she smiled, wickedly. "I'm not ready for that just yet."

Joe pushed her away, the drink spilling over her hand. "What is it going to take to be rid of you?"

She stumbled back a few steps then caught her balance. "You're not the one in control. I am."

"I'll do whatever I have to. I want this to end."

"Anything?" Mallory arched a tapered brow.

"Anything." Joe stood, his fists clenched at his sides, feet planted, muscles tensed. "I want my life back."

Mallory walked a few steps closer. "I almost hate to give you up." She rubbed a hand over his wide shoulders. "You're the best lover I've had in years," she whispered. "However, there is something I need more than great sex."

Joe's head snapped up. "What?"

"I need Sarah to sign over her shares of Dillingham Oil."

"What? Never!" Shock hardened the corners of his eyes and mouth. "She'll never do it."

"Then you need to work on her." She rubbed his shoulders. "You must persuade her."

"I can't."

"Then we shall continue our clandestine meetings." She parted his robe, her lips moving over his chest.

"No." He tried pushing her away."

She came back for more. "You know I like it rough." Mallory reached for the belt around his waist.

"Stop it." He slapped her hands away.

"Not on your life." Her blood pumped through her veins with the intensity of gushing oil. "I told you what I want. If you can't deliver, then you will deliver another way." The knot loosened, and she pulled the robe over his arms.

"I don't know how to get Sarah to agree." He struggled to pull his robe up.

"That, my dear, Joseph, isn't my problem." She reached up, capturing his lips.

He turned his head away. "Give me some time."

"Take all the time you need." She grabbed his hands, bringing them to her chest and rubbing them over the satin material.

"Stop." He pulled away. "I'm not having sex with you." He stepped back. "I'll work on a plan to get you what you want." He needed time to think. Time to figure out how to straighten out this mess.

Mallory stepped forward, closing the distance he'd created. "I don't care how long it takes for you to come up with a plan." Her husky whisper rushed past his ear. "But, we'll continue to have fun until I get Sarah's cooperation."

Joe backed up a few more steps. She seemed like an octopus. He no sooner slapped one hand away that her other hand touched him somewhere else. "Just stop." He managed to restrain both her hands. "I'm not doing this anymore."

"Yes, you are." Her foot snaked around his ankle, knocking him off balance. When he let go of her hands, she pushed him hard enough that he stumbled back. She struck his ankles once more with her foot and he fell to the floor. She landed on top of him.

"Now, let's have some fun." She ripped the straps on her teddy as she straddled him on the floor.

"No." He tried pushing her off, but she'd pinned him there.

Her lips assaulted his. Greedy. Eager. Dangerous. Bare breasts brushed against the hard muscles of his chest. Her hands roamed as her lips tasted. She moved on top of him, awaking his manhood even as he tried to stop the sensations, and she continued to rub, squeeze, kiss and play until he had no choice but to seek release.

He hated this. Hated her. Hated the fact that he couldn't control his body. Fear drove him as much as the sexual pleasure. Now, if he could only figure out how to talk Sarah into signing over her shares of the company, he would be free of Mallory. Free forever. That was all he really wanted.

Chapter 7

"There's no way I'd ever give Mallory my consent to take over Dad's company." Sarah rubbed her hands up and down her bare arm. "Why would you even suggest such a ludicrous thing?"

"I don't know." Joe sighed, sitting on the couch. He had no good reason. Since he couldn't convince himself that Mallory running the company would be a good idea, how could he ever persuade Sarah of it? His only thought centered on the smoldering look Mallory gave him at breakfast. That look usually preceded a summons to her room. It had been several days since their last encounter and he desperately wanted to avoid another one.

He hadn't even thought about what to say. He simply blurted out that Mallory would be capable of controlling the company.

"Joe." Sarah sat next him, rubbing his shoulders. "What is going on with the two of you?"

"Nothing!"

"Then why are you tensing up?" Sarah's soft voice didn't accuse, she simply wanted to help. Her gentle, loving tone soothed his tension.

"I don't know." He stood, pacing the room. "I'm just agitated, that's all."

"Is it work?"

"Yes." He walked around the room. "Things are so hectic with the new site." He stopped in front of the window and watched the birds flit around the feeders Sarah had placed there. "Mallory has been pressuring the members into her new ideas. She has some plans that just might boost the bottom line." He had to come up with some idea for pitching this bizarre notion to his wife.

"Since when do I care about money?" She stood, walking over to stand behind his broad shoulders. "When did you start caring about money?"

"When you became pregnant with my child." His shoulders dropped.

"You're really worried about becoming a dad, aren't you?"

He turned around, slipping his arms around her expanding waistline. "I want to provide the best for you and the baby."

"You're doing a fine job now." Her arms wrapped around his neck. "I care more about my family and the environment than about how much money you make." She stood on her toes and kissed his nose. "Mallory's money schemes don't interest me." Her hazel eyes searched his soul, as if trying to dig up oil that had been buried for centuries. "I don't understand why all this stuff matters to you now. You never used to care money."

"I didn't have a baby on the way and I want to provide what you're accustomed to."

"I only want your love. Nothing more."

His large arms cradled her. "You already have that."

"Then forget whatever scheme Mallory is trying to involve you in. I won't be a party to ruining the company my grandfather started."

"I'm not saying to ruin the company, but you could be helping our family."

"Where is this coming from?" She pulled out of his embrace. "Have I ever complained?" She paced a few steps away. "Are you getting self-conscious about living here, with my father? We can move out whenever you want."

"I don't want to move out. This isn't about where we live."

"Then what is it about?" Her tone sounded exasperated.

"It's about me providing for my family." He ran an agitated hand through his hair. "I would never ask you to leave your family, but I want you to consider the prospect of raising our own children. I want to provide for them on my own, and not have rely on your father for everything."

"I have done nothing but think about our family since the day I found out I was pregnant. I'd give up my life for our daughter, how dare you accuse me of not caring!"

"I didn't say you don't care." He closed the gap between them and put his hands on her shoulders. "I know how much you love this baby, and how much you love your family."

"Then how can you ask me to betray them." Tears filled her eyes. "It would break Dad's heart if Mallory gained control of the company."

"I know." Joe hugged her close. "I'm sorry, I'm being selfish." He couldn't tell her the truth. Couldn't tell her Mallory was blackmailing him. He couldn't even find the right explanation on how she got the blackmail material in the first place.

"I'm sorry, too." She hugged him back. "I know you're only trying to take care of us. I just can't do it at the expense of my dad."

"All right." Joe kissed the top of her head. He'd have to come up with some other way to get rid of Mallory.

Robert groaned as he pushed open the door then flopped down on his bed. He'd spent the day canvassing neighborhoods, knocking on doors, shaking hands and explaining his positions on the issues. He'd had debates on abortion, the war, the environment and even why hand sanitizer wasn't good for you. Doors had been slammed in his face, bad names flung at him, and on the better side, he'd got a few propositions from some very sexy women.

That brought Maria to mind. She hadn't talked to him much in the past few weeks. Their relationship seemed strained ever since Mallory threatened him with those pictures. He missed her, but he didn't have a clue how to fix things.

He loved Maria, he told her that. If he didn't, he would give in to the temptations that presented themselves on the campaign trail. Yet, even though he remained faithful, she still stayed angry with him. She wanted to get married.

Mallory made a big argument that voters wouldn't approve of his relationship with Maria because she happened to be a maid. However, most of his voters were middle income families with similar jobs. Would they really object to him marrying a maid? It seemed the only people who'd truly care were Mallory, his dad, and their wealthy friends.

A knock interrupted his thoughts.

"Maria, I was just thinking about you." He opened the door so she could step inside.

"I didn't know you were home." She held out the pile of folded towels. "I only wanted to put the clean towels away." She stood erect, shoulders squared, eyes downcast.

"Maria, will you please talk to me?"

"I don't have time. I need to finish my job so I can clock out." Her brown eyes locked with his. "I wouldn't want your voters to think you paid me overtime. They might misconstrue the meaning and use it as blackmail. Of course, they wouldn't like us being married either."

"I'm tired and I have a headache. I can't deal with this drama right now." He took the towels from her. "I'll put these away." He slammed the door. "I swear I'll never understand that women," he muttered as he walked into the bathroom.

He heard his door fly open and a jumble of Spanish words fill the air. Then, Maria stood in front of him. "Don't you ever slam a door in my face," she shouted.

"Don't speak Spanish when you're calling me names. If you're going to cuss me out do it so I can understand." He jammed the stack of towels into the cupboard and stood. "I don't even know why you're so upset."

"Because you don't love me." Tears rolled down her smooth, dark cheeks.

"Maria, I do love you," he said, gently. "I have loved you from the moment you spilled your margarita on me."

She smiled, remembering the night of her twenty-first birthday. "Your family took me and Mama to The Spanish Flowers restaurant."

"You wore a red sundress that was cut down to here." He traced a finger down her chest and stopped between the swell of her breasts.

"I'm surprised you even noticed since you were with some blond floozy."

"Oh, I remember." He smiled that devilish grin that always made her laugh. "It was the first time I noticed you'd grown up. You weren't the little bratty kid, following me around everywhere. You'd bloomed into a beautiful young woman."

"If you were in love with me, why did it take you four years to finally ask me out?" She slowly crossed her arms and arched a tapered brow in a challenge.

"I guess I was scared."

"Of me?"

"In a way. Maria, you are so beautiful and so full of life, I didn't think I had a chance with you."

"Robert, don't hand me that line." Her eyes were sharp, accessing. "You can have any woman you want. With your blue eyes, well-built body and good looks, women fall all over themselves trying to gain your attention." She let a deep sigh slip out. "I know it happens when you're out campaigning."

"Are you jealous?" He wondered if being the next state representative was worth all the hassle. "Is that what this is about?"

"No." She licked her lips. "It's about doing what's right."

"You think if I marry you, I won't cheat?"

"I'm not worried about you cheating. I trust you." She looked deep into his eyes. "How long is it going to take you to ask me to marry you?"

"I will marry you when the time is right."

"And when will that be? When I stop being a maid?"

"This has nothing to do with your job. When I ask you to be my wife it'll be because I love you, not to save my political career."

"So, until then we just keep hiding? If Mallory found out, other people are bound to guess."

"I refuse to put you in a compromising position. If we marry now, it'll look like we did it in haste. Even worse, it'll look like I was forced into it because of those stupid pictures."

"Why don't you tell Mallory to go to hell!" Maria turned, ready to flee.

Robert grabbed her arm. "Don't walk out on me."

She turned to face him, tears once again in her eyes.

"Maria," he breathed her name. "Don't cry." He wiped the tears away.

"I just don't understand. Everything was going fine. We had a plan. Then along comes your power grabbing sister and now our lives are on hold."

"It won't be for long. I'll find a way that makes everyone happy." Robert pulled her into his embrace.

"No one will be happy unless Mallory is dead."

"Maria!" He sounded shocked. He couldn't reprimand her when he'd had the same thought. But the bitterness in her tone surprised him.

Joe took a deep breath then knocked on the wooden door.

"Come in."

He knew he was entering the equivalent of the lion's den or a snake pit, but in his hands he held the deed to his freedom. He opened the door and received a crimson smile.

"Joseph, how nice to see you." Mallory stood, walked around the desk, and gave him a little too friendly of a hug. "I've been dreaming about this moment," she whispered in his ear.

"I'm sure you have." His body stiffened harder than an oil rig. "How many nights do you dream about destroying people's lives? I'd guess it's a nightly occurrence."

"Why are you always so mean?" Full, red lips pouted. "I've been nothing but generous with you." A wicked gleam glowed from her eyes, "Perhaps not enough to satisfy you." She closed and locked the door.

"Stop it." Joe slapped her hands away and held out a large, white envelope. "I have something for you."

"I'm guessing not the something I want at this moment," she sighed.

"If it's sex you want, then no." His tone could have frozen the ocean. "I have something better."

"I doubt that," she muttered. Taking the envelope she opened it and looked up sharply. "How did you get this?"

"Does it matter?"

Mallory studied the document more closely. "This isn't my sister's signature."

"Yes, it is."

"No, it's not, although it's a really good forgery."

"Then what are you complaining about."

"I need it to hold up in a court of law." She locked eyes with him. "Or else it's worthless."

"I'll make sure it holds up in court." His eyes darkened. "Besides, I'm the one that will be in trouble, not you."

"That's my point. Why are you risking so much?"

"Why aren't you accepting the papers?" He folded his large arms across his chest. "It's what you wanted. Now you will have control of Dillingham oil."

She brushed up against him.

"No." Joe pushed her back. "Sarah and the baby are my only family."

"Sarah and the baby. Sarah and the baby," she mocked. "You sound like a broken record."

"That's because you keep making me repeat myself."

"You won't admit the truth." Mallory stepped closer, whispering in his ear. "You want me."

Joe pushed her, she stumbled back a few steps. "I want you to leave me alone." He tapped the papers in her hands. "You've got what you want."

"What if I change my mind? What if I still want you?"

Joe laughed. "You'd never want anybody more than you want Dillingham oil."

"You could be wrong about that." Her voice lowered to a whisper.

Joe studied the serious look on her face for a moment then said, "No I'm not."

"You don't know me as well as you think you do."

"Yes I do." Joe took a step toward her, leaning closer he whispered, "Money, power, greed and lust. That's all you want. It's all you'll ever be capable of giving."

The words smacked Mallory with a force equal to the pressure it takes to thrust the pipes into the ground. She stiffened. "I'm not as cold and calculating as you think." Tears shimmered in her eyes. "I'm capable of love."

Joe's laugh bounced around the office. "You can stop with the wounded act. It doesn't suit you."

"Someday, Joseph Barnes, you're going to come crawling back to me." She'd give him space. Some time apart would make him realize how much he missed her. Willing her heart to slow down she looked him square in the eyes. "Someday, you'll need me."

"The only thing I want from you is that DVD."

"What?" Her mouth opened. "I'm not giving you that."

"I got you what you wanted. Now give me the DVD."

"That wasn't part of the deal."

"It is now." His brown eyes turned darker than the oil gushing from the ground. "I want that tape."

Mallory smiled. "You're not getting it. I'll leave you alone and not pressure you into sex, but the tape is my insurance policy."

"The only insurance policy you're going to need is on your life." He reached out to grab the papers in her hand, but she quickly moved out of his reach. "Don't even think about it." She walked to her desk and opened a drawer. "And don't threaten me."

"Don't play games with me." He envisioned snapping her neck like a toothpick. "I gave you everything you wanted."

"Not everything," she said under her breath. She locked the desk then held up the key. Slowly, with seductive movements she slid the key down her blouse.

Joe watched as the silver key disappeared into the sea of blue silk. "This isn't over." Joe stomped to the door.

"Not by a long shot." She yelled as the door slammed shut.

Mallory barged into the meeting looking like a panther in her black pants suit. "Sorry I'm so late." She apologized with a triumphant smile.

Richard stopped talking and frowned at his daughter. It wasn't like her to be late. He'd always joked that she was so punctual you could tell the time by her movements. This huge disturbance didn't fit with her personality either.

Richard waited for her to take her seat, but she walked up to the front and stood beside him. "Father, we have some important business to discuss. You may want to take a seat." She pulled out his chair.

"Mallory will you stop fooling around and sit down so I can proceed with the meeting." Richard said, irritated.

"We are proceeding with the meeting, however, I am taking charge." She set her briefcase on the table. The latches clicked open then she withdrew a folder and handed it to her father. "If you read through this, you'll see I have everything in order."

"What the ..."

"It's time we had some new, innovated ideas." She cut Richard off. "The only way we can bring about change is to have someone heading the company who is fearless. Someone willing to take chances." She paused. "I believe there is a way to increase our profits. However, it requires an intelligent and knowledgeable person with guts." She raised a fisted hand into the air. "I believe I am the person for the job."

She looked each stockholder in the eye. "I have already mailed everyone a letter detailing my complaints against the president and documented my plan to bring Dillingham Oil into the twenty-first century.

Mallory paused long enough to notice her father's face turn from a pale white into a deep red. "Now, I must confess that this hasn't been an easy decision for me. I admit that it's hard to oust the company's president when he's my father." She glanced at Richard once more, ignoring the hurt and disbelief in his eyes. "I've thought long and hard about this, but it comes down to one thing: what is best for the company?"

She paced around the table. "As hard as it is for me to wrestle the company away from my own parent, it became increasingly clear that this is the only way we'd ever see change." She walked back to her briefcase as Richard slowly sank into his chair. Mallory pulled out a stack of papers. "John Colthrop, would you be a dear and pass these out for me?"

The young man sitting to her left stood and took the papers. After distributing them to each member he sat back down, and Mallory continued. "The first item is to update our equipment. We cannot compete in today's market without the technology of this century. Oil rigs and other equipment are making great strides using computers. We need to take advantage of this or we'll be left behind, pumping the equivalence of buckets of oil while everyone else is pumping barrels.

"I know the new oil rig is expensive but if you'll look at page three, I've mapped out the projection numbers over the next three years." She waited while everyone looked over the information. "The rig will pay itself off, and start turning a profit in a couple years.

"Now, as most of you will remember, a report by the Texas Railroad Commission last year showed that Texas is producing twenty-nine percent of America's natural gas. Our oil production was 337 million barrels for the year. Our state ranking of crude oil is 1,088,000 barrels a day."

"Mallory we know all this, why are you wasting time rehashing old figures?" Richard barked. "Now, stop this nonsense."

"It's not nonsense." Malory glowered. "I bring this point up because analysts have shown that the world market is flat."

"So-called experts predicted the end of the oil age for more than a hundred years. You can't believe that crap," Richard said.

"On page six you'll find a list of important facts that can't be ignored." She held up her index finger. "One, the Oil and Gas journal showed that worldwide oil production was 66.7 million barrels a day in 2001. The production only slightly increased to 68 million barrels a day by 2003. She held up a second finger. "The report also says that the world used four times as much oil as was found in 2002." She held up a third finger. "And, the discovery of new oil sites has slowed down. Sixteen large discoveries were reported in 2000, eight in 2001, and only three in 2003, with none being reported at all last year."

Mallory slammed her hands down on the table. "The time for action is now. Companies are drilling fewer and fewer wells each year. Our existing wells are slowing down and soon they'll dry up. If we don't start looking at new ideas Dillingham Oil is going to be left in the dust."

"The reason companies are drilling less wells is because new scientific advances have increased the production, so they don't have to drill as many wells to get the same amount of barrels per day." John Colthorp clarified.

"Exactly!" Mallory shouted. "That's my point. We aren't trying new scientific methods, or using computer technology. We need to change more than our methods of drilling, we need new locations. If everyone will turn to page ten, you'll see some innovated ideas for drilling in Alaska and the Gulf of Mexico."

"Everyone knows the risk is too great for drilling in those places," Richard said. "We've discussed all of these points before."

"No, Father. I brought them up and you said no. You don't listen to anything new." Mallory crossed her arms. "If everyone has turned there, I'll continue." She took a deep breath and launched into the benefits of deep sea drilling and drilling in Libya, should the government lift the bans on that desert nation. She then talked about their neighbor in Irving Texas that had started drilling in Oooguruk, Alaska. "As larger basins of oil become harder to find we have to consider alternative solutions. Oooguruk has the potential of yielding 90 million barrels of oil."

"But its three miles offshore in the Atlantic Ocean," Richard grumbled. "Do you know the time and the cost of bringing in truckloads of gravel and building an island to set the rig on?"

"It says here it was over 500 million dollars." Stanley whistled.

"Their profits were $750 million." Mallory pointed out.

"But it's a huge gamble," Richard repeated. "Dillingham will go bust if we invested that much money into one project and something happened."

"And we'll go bust if we sit around here doing nothing." Mallory stared her father down. "I'm not about to let this company get ruined because you're scared to take a gamble. It's a risk to do nothing."

"Not to mention the oil is piped under the ocean, that's a catastrophe waiting to happen," Justin Walker added.

"Mallory, is that the end of your complaints against the president?" Walter asked.

"Yes, I say it's high time we vote in a leader that isn't weak and old fashioned."

"What is your new plan?" Justin asked.

"First of all, we need a change in leadership. I will appoint John Colthrop as V.P. and William Moss will advance to chief financial officer. Walter Bishop will be chief executive, and I of course, will take over as president." She tugged on the bottom of her jacket. "After all, we need to keep the company in the Dillingham family."

"Then why doesn't Robert take over?" Another member wanted to know.

"My brother's heart lies elsewhere. You all know he's busy trying to live up to his name, bright and fame. He can only achieve that through politics." The corners of her mouth tilted in a sly smile. "Besides, I'm the one with guts enough to change this company."

"Can we get on with the vote? I'm tired of hearing her brag about herself," Justin complained.

"I make a motion to vote Mallory Dillingham in as president, immediately taking over the duties of Dillingham Oil Corporation." Mallory stood tall. "All in favor raise your hand." She raised hers and looked around the room.

John and Walter raised their hands. Mallory looked at Justin and he unhappily raised his too. Lastly, Robert, painstaking raised his hand.

Richard's face hardened like granite, but his eyes showed his hurt and unbelief that his own children would turn against him. "That's only five, not enough to carry the vote," he said.

Mallory pulled out a sheet of paper. "My sister, Sarah was unable to make the meeting but she's signed over her consent and shares to me." She handed Richard the paper with a triumphant smile. "That makes six. Since all three of us kids own twelve percent that gives me a total of fifty-five percent in shares, more than enough to pass."

The commotion in the room roared into a shouting match as other members screamed at the ones who'd participated in this coup. How could Mallory, of all people, be president? No one could make any sense of this situation.

"Don't worry, Richard, we'll fight this in court," some of his friends said before they left. But Richard wasn't listening. He sat alone in his chair at the head of the table. He stayed there for several hours, staring into the darkness, letting the bleakness seep into his soul.

Chapter 8

"Mrs. Santiago, get me some champagne," Mallory bellowed and slammed the refrigerator door shut. She put a hand behind her neck, turning it from side to side trying to work the kinks out. "Why hasn't anything gone my way since the takeover?" she asked aloud.

The meeting had ended in so much chaos that she slipped out quietly to head home, but the traffic had been backed up and the normal forty-five minute drive had taken an hour and a half. And, to top it off, no one had been home to greet her or congratulate her on the greatest accomplishment of a lifetime.

"Why isn't the bar fridge stocked?" She grumbled as the maid appeared in the doorway.

"Sorry, Miss Dillingham, I haven't had time to bring any up from the basement."

"It's your job to keep this place running smoothly. If you can't handle that, maybe it's time for you to leave. You can take that lazy, no good daughter with you." Mallory watched the wrinkles around the old maid's eyes deepen. "Things will be changing around here soon, and you can bet I'm not going to be as lenient as my father."

The pop of the cork broke the hostility in the room.

"I'll do a better job, ma'am." Mrs. Santiago poured the bubbling liquid into a crystal fluted glass.

"See that you do." Mallory sipped the champagne, the bubbles tickling her nose while exploding on her tongue. The stress of the day dissolved like ice in lemonade on a hot summers' day. "You'd better have a talk with Maria too."

"Yes, ma'am." The clipped retort was followed by a swift exit.

Mallory poured another glass and let the excitement of the day course through her body. It intoxicated her more than the alcohol in her glass. She didn't want to be alone getting drunk.

Her first thought turned to Joseph, even if in gaining control of the company she'd had to let him go. What a pity too, her body craved his touch. She knew William would be happy to celebrate with her, after all he'd organized most of this, but now that she had Dillingham Oil she didn't need him. She felt ecstatic about not having to please that toad of a man anymore. All the oil in the world would have to disappear before she had sex with him again.

John Colthrop came to mind. Her body immediately started responding to the image of the young buck with brown hair and black eyes. He certainly exuded stamina and sexual attraction. She guessed that was why he'd voted with her. That was the main reason she'd made him vice president of the company.

Mallory picked up the phone and dialed the maid service. "Maria, get me John Colthrop on the phone." A few minutes later she was flirting with the deep voice on the other end of the line.

"I just thought maybe the new V.P. would want to celebrate with the new president. After all, we just pulled off the biggest coup d'état since Abdel Aziz ousted Abdallahi in Mauritania, Africa."

Richard tossed the keys onto his desk and sank down into the brown leather chair. He'd only been home ten minutes when Maria appeared at the door.

"Mr. Dillingham, may I have a word with you?"

"Sure," he sighed.

Maria hesitantly stepped closer. "If this is a bad time, it can wait until later."

"No, might as well hear it now, besides I doubt things can get any worse."

"It's about my mother."

"Is she sick?" Richard asked.

"No." Maria tucked some curly strands of hair behind her ear. "But she's being mistreated and it's not fair."

"I see." Richard winced. "I can only guess who's doing the mistreating."

"I don't want to speak ill of your children, sir, especially since I grew up here with them, but one of your offspring is nothing short of ruthless."

"Mallory?" Richard's eyes dropped down to look at the photograph sitting on the corner of his desk. His three children looked back at him with teenage youthfulness and an innocent zeal. How had Mallory's path detoured so much?

"She's threatened my mother several times. Always yelling at her, saying she's not doing a good job, calling her and me lazy." Maria's tone went up an octave. "I don't really care what she says about me, but my mom has worked her fingers raw caring for this family. Her whole life has been dedicated to you. I won't stand for her being treated this way. Please, Mr. Dillingham, you must do something."

"I know how hard Mrs. Santiago works. I will take care of this situation."

"Maria, why are you bothering Mr. Dillingham?" Mrs. Santiago's sharp protest came from the doorway.

"Mama." Maria turned and watched her mother walk across the room, hands resting on her hips, dark eyes narrowed and a pinched expression that let Maria know a scolding was coming. "I'm not bothering him. I wanted to inform him what Mallory has been up to."

"Mr. Dillingham knows what his children are up to just like I know what you're up to."

"And what am I up to?" Maria crossed her arms under her chest, lifting her pointed nose slightly. "I am defending you."

"I do not need you to defend me." Mrs. Santiago pointed to her chest. "I am the parent and I don't need you stirring up trouble." She looked at Richard. "I am sorry my daughter has been bothering you. I will see that it never happens again."

"Maria isn't bothering me. She did bring something to my attention and I wish to speak to you about it."

"Yes, sir." Mrs. Santiago let out an explosion of Spanish directed at Maria.

Maria responded with her own Spanish then stomped out of the room.

"You were a little harsh with her, don't you think?" Richard raised a bushy brow. "She was seeing to it that you got treated fairly."

"Children must learn when to draw the line. She overstepped and must be brought up for it."

"Perhaps that's where I went wrong with Mallory. Was I too soft with her? Did I not love her enough?" His deep voice turned thick with emotion.

"Mr. Dillingham, you can't blame yourself. You are a wonderful father. Maybe the loss of her mother has affected her judgment."

"I can't blame anyone but myself."

"But you raised the other two children, and they are wonderful, loving and selfless."

Richard laughed, a harsh, hard laugh. "All three of my children have turned against me."

"No." Mrs. Santiago looked stunned. "Surely not Sarah."

"Yes. My princess and my only son both sided with Mallory. She now controls the company."

"What? No!" She found a chair and sank down in it. "I don't understand. How? Why?"

"I don't have the answers." He walked over to the window and stared out into the darkness. "You should be grateful that your daughter loves you enough to try and protect you."

"Your children love you also."

"They have a strange way of showing it."

Mrs. Santiago stood and walked over to the cabinet, pouring some brandy into a glass. "Mr. Dillingham, I have worked in this house since you and Mrs. Dillingham were married. I helped with each baby when they came home from the hospital. I watched them grow into adults and I know without a doubt that they love you."

"Even Mallory?" Richard turned around.

"Even Mallory," she reassured him. "Mallory is just too ambitious for her own good."

"I know." He sighed. "But I can't come up with any reasons why Sarah and Robert would turn against me."

"I can't either, but I'm sure there is an explanation." She walked over, handing him the drink. "Why don't you get some sleep, perhaps things will look brighter in the morning."

"Thanks." Richard drank half the liquid in one gulp. "I don't think I'll be able to sleep." He finished the drink. "However, a few more of these should help."

"Where's Dad?" Sarah asked as she set her plate down.

"I don't know." Joe reached over and stole a strip of bacon off her plate.

"He's usually the first one up. He missed dinner last night too." The small lines around her eyes deepened. "I wonder if he's feeling well."

"Sarah, honey, there's something you need to know." Joe exhaled, loudly. "Your sister took control of the company yesterday."

"What!" Sarah threw her napkin down on the table. "How did she manage that?"

"I don't have all the details."

"Dad must be devastated." Sarah sat down. "How could she do that to him?" She shook her head. "I can't understand how this happened."

"Take it easy, Sarah. Don't get yourself worked up. You don't want to endanger the baby." Joe reached over and intertwined his large fingers with her small ones.

"The baby's fine." Sarah stood. "My dad, on the other hand is not." Tears slipped down her cheeks. "Where's Mallory?" She withdrew her hand from Joe and started toward the door.

"Sarah, please calm down." Joe went after her. "The doctor said you shouldn't get upset."

"Upset!" She started up the winding staircase. "Mallory has just ripped my family apart, I'm more than upset."

"Think about the baby," he begged.

But Sarah stormed up the stairs and down the hallway. When she got to Mallory's door, she barged

104

right in, not even knocking. "Where is that traitor?" She yelled after noticing the bed was empty.

"I don't know, Mrs. Barnes, she didn't come home last night." The maid informed her.

"She's probably out prowling around, gloating no doubt." Sarah wiped the tears off her cheeks. "She won't get away with this." Sarah grabbed her abdomen, doubling over.

"What's wrong?" Joe asked.

"I have a sharp pain."

Joe picked her up. "Get our bed ready," he ordered.

The maid ran down the stairs and into their bedroom. Joe followed close behind. "Get Richard."

"What's wrong?" Richard ran into the room, his shabby appearance more unsettling than his urgent tone.

"Sarah's having pains," Joe said.

Richard went to the bed.

"Dad, how did Mallory get control of your company?"

"Don't worry about the company now." He sat on the edge of the bed. "How are you feeling?"

"I have a bad headache and my vision is a little blurry." Sarah sat back against the pillows. "I want to know how she did it," Sarah insisted.

Richard rubbed his hands down his face, exhaling loudly. "You should know how she did it. You signed your shares over to her."

"I never did that." Sarah jerked up, grabbing his hand. "Please believe me, Dad. I'd never betray you like that."

Richard looked confused. "I saw your signature."

"Maybe Mallory forged my name." She grabbed her head, moaning.

"Get the car, we need to get her to the hospital," Richard yelled.

Mallory stalked across the room, miffed that for the second day in a row no one was around to greet her.

"Where is everyone?" She poured herself a drink.

"At the hospital. Sarah is having problems." Mrs. Santiago hung Mallory's coat in the closet.

"Of course," Mallory sneered. "I do something sensational so she has to have a problem."

"Your sister is having complications with her baby. I don't think she's doing it on purpose just to upstage you."

"Don't take that tone with me." Her blue eyes slanted. "Now I'm going to have to go to the hospital and waste my time playing the dutiful sister. Of all the most inconvenient times."

"I don't think your family wants you there, so don't bother with your acting skills."

"You are nothing but a servant. I won't put up with your disrespect." She took a sip of her drink.

"If you want respect, you need to earn it."

"You're fired. And take that money grabbing daughter with you."

"You have no power to fire me." Mrs. Santiago crossed her arms. "You may have stolen the company, but you will never take over this house."

"We'll see about that." Mallory laughed.

"I feel sorry for you."

"Why, I have everything I ever wanted."

"At what cost? You've pushed your family out of your life."

"I don't need anyone. I depend on myself and I like it that way."

"Your mother would be broken hearted to see how cold you've become."

"Funny, I talked to her last week and she didn't say a word." She downed the rest of the drink. "Tombstones don't talk."

"Nothing gets to you, does it?"

"No." Mallory stared at her. "I like it that way."

"You're a sad, lost, lonely little girl."

"I'm not a girl."

Mrs. Santiago walked to the door then turned and said, "I wonder how different you would be if your mother hadn't died."

"This has nothing to do with my mother." Mallory threw her drink against the wall. The shattering glass silenced her sob.

Joe paced the waiting room, his bulky frame tensed and agitated. Richard sat silently wedged into a chair. The last few hours had crawled by with unbelievable slowness. Finally an elderly man with gray hair and a white lab coat came into the room.

"Dr. Burton," Richard stood. "How are Sarah and the baby?"

"Her blood pressure is too high and I'm concerned about the high levels of cortisone in her system." The doctor flipped a page on the clipboard. "She also has some swelling in her ankles and wrists."

"What's that mean?" Joe asked.

"They're symptoms of pregnancy-induced hypertension or PIH. I've started her on an intravenous of Labetalol for the blood pressure. I'm still running some tests on the baby, but right now they both seem stable."

"Preeclampsia - isn't that what Margaret had?" Richard's face paled.

"Your wife's case developed into eclampsia. Now, it is true that PIH tends to run in the family and that women whose mothers or sisters had it are three times more likely to get it, but it is still very rare. Eclampsia occurs in about one in 1,600 pregnancies and usually develops towards the end. Sarah is strong and only at twenty-six weeks. She has plenty of time to bring down her blood pressure."

"What do we need to do?" Joe's matter of fact tone belied how scared he felt inside. Sarah's mother had died giving birth to her. He couldn't live a life without Sarah. He wondered how Richard had done it all these years.

"As I said, I have her on medicine to bring down her blood pressure. She's going to have to stay in bed and watch her diet. Plus, limit the salt intake."

"Sarah's always been a healthy eater," Richard said.

"Good, that will make things easier." Dr. Burton slipped his glasses on. "One more thing, she has to limit the stress in her life. If her sugar and blood pressure spike this high again she may go into seizures."

"Thanks, Dr. Burton." Richard shook his hand.

"Don't worry she's going to be fine. I won't allow eclamscia to take another Dillingham."

"One more thing." Joe stopped the doctor as he started to leave. "Will the medicine hurt the baby?"

"No. But I do need to caution you that the baby isn't as big as I'd like."

"Is that a serious problem?"

"It can be towards the end of the pregnancy and during delivery. Right now I'm cautiously concerned. There is time for the baby to gain enough weight before delivery, but I can't stress how important it is for Sarah to remain off her feet and calm. If her stress level doesn't decrease both she and the baby can be in serious danger."

"I understand," Joe assured the doctor.

Richard walked over and clasped Joe's shoulder. "Don't worry we'll take good care of her." He looked Joe in the eyes. "Nothing is going to happen to Sarah or my grandchild, I'll personally see to it."

Joe watched Sarah shift positions in the bed. Her eyes slowly opened. "Hey." She sounded weak, tired.

"Hey." Joe smiled. "How do you feel?"

"Like I've been hit by a truck." She sat up.

Joe poured her a glass of water and handed it to her.

"Thanks." She drank it down. "How do you always know what I want before I even ask?"

"I don't know," he sighed. "Maybe it's telepathy."

Sarah ran her fingers through her short, honey brown hair. "I must look awful."

"You look beautiful." Joe leaned over and kissed her. "As beautiful as the day we first met."

"You're lying, but that's why I love you so much."

"I remember following your dad through the house. We stopped in the hallway and I looked into the dining room and saw you sitting at the table, papers sprawled out all over. The sun looked as if it was dancing in your hair, then you looked up at me and I melted on the spot."

"Is that when you fell in love with me?"

"Actually, no. I fell in love with you half an hour later, when you barged into your dad's office, waving papers and arguing that we had to use safer environmentally friendly drilling fluids and that a chemical company was producing fluids based on high performance vegetable oil technology."

"I want to preserve the land." Sarah's eyes filled with tears. "Now with Mallory running the company, wanting to drill in Alaska we could have another major oil spill like back in 1989. Do you remember when that tanker struck the reef and spilled eleven million gallons of oil?"

"I do."

"And what about in 2010? That BP explosion in the Gulf of Mexico not only killed 11 people but was the worst oil spill in history. Do you know how much oil leaked into the Gulf? 4.9 million barrels. Do you know how much devastation it caused?" Her round face flushed red.

"I know. I know." Joe used a quiet tone, trying to calm her down. "But you need to take care of our baby right now. No more work or worrying until after she is born."

"I'm sorry. I didn't mean to get so worked up." Sarah took a couple deep breaths. "I promise to be good."

"I love you." Joe leaned over to kiss her pink lips gently. "Now get some rest."

Mallory waltzed into the room, her purple duster flying behind her like a witch's cape. "Well, it's about time someone finally came home."

"Why, did you miss us?" Richard's tone sounded tight, forced.

"I just wanted to know how poor, dear Sarah is doing." Ice cubes clanked in the glass.

"She's doing fine." Richard sighed. "However, she's going to need to take it easy and needs to reduce the stress in her life."

"What stress?" Mallory poured some scotch into her glass. "She doesn't do anything to get stressed about. Oh, wait! Is it that stressful trying to save the environment?" Mallory laughed. "I'm sure saving all those endangered species is so tiring. Maybe if she let up on lecturing us about the oil fields damaging the environment she'd be stress free."

"That's enough!" Richard's sharp tone bounced off the crystal glass in Mallory hand and the chandelier above them. "Just because your sister is on the opposite side as you, doesn't mean her work isn't important. Her work is just as fulfilling as yours."

"Oh, please!" Mallory rolled her eyes. "Environmentalists are nothing but a pain in the ass." She sipped her drink. "You know it as well as I do. They're always complaining about something."

"Sarah has done some good work." Richard strained to keep control of his emotions. "Her company started the Rigs To Reefs program and look how successful it is."

"So what? They cut off the tops of old rigs and leave the bottoms in the water for fish to swim in. I never got what is so important about inventing playhouses for fish."

"You never understand anything."

"Maybe I just don't care."

"And that's the biggest problem." Richard looked at his daughter, regret edging his words. "You don't care about anything except money and power."

"What else is there?"

"Family, loyalty, trust and love. Why are these things so foreign to you?"

"I don't know, maybe because I don't care."

"That poses a big problem." Richard's gaze hardened. "I think it would be best if you moved closer to the office."

"You've got to be kidding." Mallory's eyes hardened. "You're kicking me out of the house."

"The drive from Galveston to Houston is a killer. I think an apartment closer to the office will serve you better."

"This has nothing to do with my convenience. You're just mad because the all mighty king Richard has been dethroned." Taking a sip of her drink, she looked her dad in the eyes. "You know, just because your name means rich and powerful, that doesn't mean everyone is going to bow and kiss your hand."

"It's not just me. I have other family members to protect."

"Oh, I see. This is about Sarah. Once again I get tossed aside for your little princess." She downed the rest of her drink in one gulp. "And you wonder why I don't feel like a part of this family."

"You are the one who's made this mess. You've pushed everyone away with no thought to anyone's feelings." Richard pointed his finger in her face. "You have destroyed any love and trust I've ever placed in you." His voice cracked. "I can't trust you not to hurt other people and I need to protect my family."

"This isn't fair!" Mallory threw her glass at him.

He ducked and it smashed into a vase of flowers. He shook his head and walked out of the room.

Chapter 9

"Hey, Princess how are you feeling?" Richard kissed the top of Sarah's head.

"I'd be better if everyone stopped hovering."

"We're only concerned," Joe said.

"I know. I'm just feeling grumpy." She sighed. "I don't want to be confined to bed."

"Sweetheart, it's best for the baby." Joe laced his fingers through hers. "We want to make sure you're comfortable."

"Is the bell really necessary?"

"Yes," Mrs. Santiago answered as she entered the room, carrying a tray. "Ring it and someone will come." She set the tray by the bed. "I made some lemon herbal tea."

"Thanks."

"I have the schedule for your medication and I'm working on the new menu."

"I hate to be so much trouble."

Mrs. Santiago squeezed her hand. "It's no trouble. We're all going to take care of you and the baby. Stop fretting and rest."

"I'll try."

"Good girl." Mrs. Santiago handed her a cup of tea. "Drink up." With that she left.

"I have some business to finish before dinner." Richard kissed Sarah then clapped Joe on the back. "Take care of my girls."

"I will, sir."

Maria ignored Robert as he attempted to kiss her.

"What now?" His sigh was heavy, longing.

"Why haven't you told your father about Mallory blackmailing you?"

"Because I don't want him to know, that's the whole point of blackmail. You do what the blackmailer says to keep the information hidden."

"Do you ever plan on telling him?"

"Yes, but not now."

"When? After the election? After you become senator, governor, or maybe after you become president?"

"Will you quit fighting me and let me handle this my own way?"

"What about your dad?" She looked at him with a tear stained face. "He thinks you betrayed him. Are you just going to let him think that?"

"I did betray him." Robert fought back tears of regret. "The reason for doing so isn't going to change anything."

"It could make a difference."

"He'll never forgive me."

"You won't know until you tell him the whole story."

"Not right now." Robert buried his face into her hair, hugging her tight. "Just stay with me and give me some time to figure things out."

"I love you Robert."

"And I love you."

The April sun beat down on Joe and his crew. He wiped his brow and wished he could take his shirt off and dry up the river running down his back, but the white pick-up bouncing over the field warned him of Mallory's arrival.

The roughnecks and derrickhands whistled and catcalled as she got out of the truck. Mallory waved, put her yellow hard hat and safety glasses on, then headed toward Joe.

"What do you want?" Joe jumped off the last rung of the ladder, landing on the ground with a thud.

"Don't take that tone with me."

"You disrupt the crew every time you come out here. How am I supposed to get any work done when the guys are staring at you?"

"That's not my problem, you're the driller. It's your job to control the crew." Mallory stepped closer. "Are you jealous?"

"Hardly," Joe snorted.

"Do you miss me?" Inching closer, she rubbed her breasts against his chest.

"Stop it!" Joe pushed her and she stumbled back a few steps.

"You don't expect to hold me to that stupid contract, do you?"

"Absolutely." Joe's eyes hardened.

"We could renegotiate the terms."

"Leave me alone."

Mallory moved forward with more determination than before. "You can say no with your mouth, but your eyes tell me you miss me as much as I miss you." She brushed against him once more, wrapping her arms around his neck. "It's been several weeks since we had sex and your body is screaming with desire."

"Neither my body nor my eyes are saying anything to you except get away." He unwound her arms and shoved her so hard she fell to the ground. "Can't you show any decency?"

"That's what you love about me." Mallory stood, wiping dirt of her butt. "You love the way I make you feel. I don't care about respectability or being proper. I'm wild and exciting. Rules don't mean anything and that makes me unpredictable, unlike little boring, predicable Sarah."

"I hate you, Mallory Dillingham. When are you going to realize that? You don't know the meaning of love." His stare nailed her heart. "Stay away from me and Sarah." He walked over to the ladder and started climbing up to the platform.

Mallory went up the ladder too. "You aren't walking away from me." She followed him into his office slamming the door behind her. "I won't be ignored."

"Unfortunately." Joe sighed.

"I'm your boss."

"You're a pain in my..."

Mallory knocked Joe off balance and pushed him against the wall, then flung her body against his chest, savagely kissing him.

"Stop!" Joe pushed at her.

"Hey, boss." The office door opened and a young man stopped abruptly. "*Oh.*"

"Damn," Joe breathed and pushed Mallory away. "What's wrong?"

"Umm, the pipe is jammed."

Joe followed the derrickman out to the platform. The loud *ding, ding, ding* of the hammer pounding on the stuck pipe filled the derrick.

Mallory followed, miffed that the crew went to Joe instead of her. She watched as Joe shouted out orders, which the crew quickly followed with no complaints.

"What's wrong?" Mallory asked.

"One of the connections must have come loose," Joe said.

"Or the pipe may have hit rock." The floor hand suggested.

"How fast were they drilling?" Joe asked. "We need to pump slower. We're not drilling that deep, only about medium radius." Joe checked some printouts. "I think we need more fluids pumped into the crack."

"Why so much fluid?" Mallory asked. She tried to sound serious, but all the talk of holes, pumping and fluid had her own fluids pumping.

"We're using the stimulation technology." Joe ignored the smile spreading across her face.

"I love your stimulation technology," she whispered loudly over the banging.

"Mallory, you need to leave." Joe walked over to the pipe.

"You can't tell me what to do."

"You don't know what you're doing on the rig. You'll get hurt."

"I'm a big girl and can handle myself."

"Bill," Joe called. "Climb up on the derrick and start guiding the pipe. We're gonna bring up a few pieces and see if we can find an angle that isn't tight."

"Sure thing, boss." Bill left to get his safety harness on.

A couple of roughnecks got ready to bring the long pieces of pipe up. Although Mallory wouldn't leave the platform, she did stand out of the way. As the drill brought up the pieces of pipe, muddy water splattered all over the deck. She cussed as her feet got soaked. She wanted to leave at that point, but didn't want to look weak.

The roughnecks worked to bring the pipe out of the ground while the derrickman stood about fifty feet above them. He hauled the thirty foot lengths of pipe using cables. After a few pieces of pipe had been brought up, Mallory started to enjoy watching the rhythm of the men.

Even though the men were wet and muddy, she still liked watching their muscles flex beneath their T-shirts as they strained against the machinery. She couldn't help but admire the roundness of their backsides as they bent over, but mostly, she watched Joe. The way he stayed calm and in control. His leadership and knowledge were well known around Texas. He'd worked up through the ranks from roughneck to driller in a relatively short amount of time.

He'd dated and married Sarah rather quickly, too; everything about him felt fast. Surprisingly, he was slow and unhurried in bed.

"Watch out!" The shout penetrated her thoughts and Mallory looked up to see a large pipe falling toward her.

She screamed and lunged out of the way as the pipe hit the platform with an ear shattering thud. She felt the metal floor vibrate, then felt her body being pulled down. In horror she realized that she'd rolled off the end of the platform. In desperation her hands flung out, grabbing hold of something hard and sharp.

"Help me!" She yelled. She held on to the edge of the floor, the metal cutting into her hands.

Joe started toward her then stopped. He looked down at her dangling twenty-five above the ground. His life would be so much simpler if she were gone.

"Joe, I can't hold on much longer." Mallory caught the look in his eyes. "Please," she begged.

The note of desperation spurred him into action. He reached down and hauled her up.

Once she stood firmly on the platform, she looked at him, rubbing her bruised and bloodied hands. "It took you long enough."

"You're lucky I saved your worthless life at all." He walked away.

Mallory replayed the scene on the oil rig over and over. She'd almost died and no one seemed to care. Her father had made her move out over two weeks ago and not one family member bothered to call or ask how she was doing. Joseph had been tempted to let her die.

"Surely they can't all be that selfish and heartless," she stated out loud. After pouring a drink, she went to take a shower. "Maybe I'll drive over to the house for dinner."

The murmur of voices and the clatter of silverware stopped when she walked in.

"Hello, everyone, what's for dinner?"

"Mallory." Richard stood. "I didn't know you were joining us."

"Do I need an invitation?" She walked over to her usual place. "I am still a member of this family." Pulling out the chair, she sat. "I mean Robert and Sarah signed over their shares and they'll still here."

Robert glared at her.

"I never said you weren't part of the family." Richard also took a seat. "I hear you had an accident on the rig."

"Yes, but Joe saved me." She winked him. "Speaking of accidents how is Sarah?"

"She's fine," Joe said.

"Good." Mallory smiled as the maid placed her food on the table. "Steak tartare, my favorite."

After dessert, Mallory asked to see Sarah.

"Not a good idea," Joe said.

"But she's my sister. I want to see how she's doing." Mallory held up a pink bag. "Besides I brought something for the baby."

Joe hesitated. He wanted to keep Mallory as far away from Sarah as possible, and yet he knew having some company and a surprise gift would cheer his wife up. "Sarah can't have any stress right now."

"I promise it'll be a stress free visit." Mallory crossed her heart with her finger. "I want to make amends."

"Let me see if she's awake."

A few minutes later Mallory was sitting in Sarah's bedroom. The tension was thick, but both parties were trying to salvage something from their relationship.

"How are you feeling?" Mallory asked.

"Like an inflated beach ball." Sarah struggled to sit up.

"Let me help you." Joe rushed over to arrange the pillows behind her.

"I'm fine," Sarah playfully swatted is hand away.

"Here, let me help." Mallory stood and fluffed the pillows.

"I'm not an invalid," Sarah grumbled.

"Of course not." Mallory sat back down. "But you deserve to be pampered. After all you are giving Joe his first child, Dad his first grandchild, and me, my first niece so let us do something for you."

"I'm sorry I didn't mean to be so unkind. I'm just tired of staying in bed, watching T.V. or reading."

"Well, maybe this will help." Mallory held up the bag. "I got a little something for you and the baby."

Sarah didn't reach out for the bag. She looked at Joe.

Mallory's fake smile faded. "Sarah, I know things have been strained between us but I want to make it up to you."

"By giving me a present?"

"What about an apology?" She smiled again. "I'm sorry."

"It's a start," Sarah admitted. "But I don't think it's enough."

"What can I do?"

"Give Dad his company back."

"Sarah, that's the one thing I can't do. But I do want to try and move on. We are still family after all."

"I just don't understand how you could do something so deceitful."

"I had business reasons, Sarah. It really wasn't personal."

"How can you say that?" Sarah's voice started to rise.

"Honey, maybe Mallory should come back another time," Joe said.

"No, I'm fine." She took a couple deep breaths then smiled at Joe. "All better."

Joe looked skeptical.

"All right, no more business talk. I'm not here to cause trouble. I want to give you a small token as a way of starting over." Mallory held up the bag. "Let's forget the past and start over new."

Sarah eyed her sister. "I don't know if that's possible."

"Anything is possible if you put your heart into it."

"Well," Sarah watched her sister's face, and didn't see any trace of malice. Maybe Mallory really missed them and wanted to truly make atonement. "I am dying to see what's in the bag."

"Good." Mallory handed her the gift with a flourish.

"Oh, Mallory, it's gorgeous." Sarah pulled out a box with a gold charm bracelet.

"I can add charms to it as the baby grows. They have golden booties for her first steps and even a tooth for when she loses her first one." Mallory pointed out a few charms on it now. "That's her first pacifier, here's a book for her first story book."

"She doesn't have a pacifier or book yet," Sarah said.

"Keep looking in the bag."

Sarah pulled out a pacifier and a Mother Goose book of poems. "How sweet."

"The egg is for the night she was conceived," Mallory said.

"Mallory!" Sarah laughed. "That's so bad."

"Yes, but that's me." Mallory laughed and hugged Sarah. "I really want to be a good aunt."

"You will be."

Joe stood at the foot of the bed, looking intimidating. Mallory was up to something, he just couldn't figure out what. As the women chatted, he realized that Sarah had already forgiven Mallory. The two talked as if nothing had happened. But that was Sarah, always forgiving and trusting. She looked for the good in people. It seemed beyond her comprehension that evil people existed.

"Honey, could you get something to drink?" Sarah smiled. "Maybe some Ginger Ale, my stomach is hurting a little."

"Sure." He left in a hurry.

"He won't be gone long but that will at least give us a few minutes alone," Sarah said.

"Good." Mallory smiled. "His hovering is making me nervous."

"His heart is in the right place. He's only trying to protect me."

"You'd think he would do a better job." Mallory's tone turned accusing. "I mean, cheating on you isn't exactly helping."

Sarah furrowed her brow. "What are you talking about?"

"He's been having sex with someone else." Mallory raised her tapered brow. "Didn't he tell you?"

Sarah looked dazed. "You're lying."

"Am I?" Mallory reached into the pink bag and fumbled around with the tissue paper. She pulled out some photographs. "Here's the proof."

Sarah took the pictures, her hand trembling as her eyes focused on the images. Joe and Mallory kissing. Her husband ripping the dress off her sister's body. The two of them doing intimate things that he should only be doing with her.

She inhaled sharply. Tears filled her eyes. "How could you?"

"I'm sorry you had to find out this way, but it's for the best. You'd have found out sooner or later. I figured the sooner the better. I mean, you don't want to drag this marriage out when he's in love with me."

"You slut!" Sarah screamed, her heart breaking. She grabbed her stomach. "Get out! Get out! I never want to see you again." She moaned and withered on the bed. "I hate you!"

Joe rushed into the room, Ginger Ale sloshing over the rim of the glass. "Sarah, what's wrong?" He looked into her grief stricken face, then noticed the pictures spread out on the bed. "Sarah, I ..."

"Shut up!" She put her hands over her ears. "I don't want to hear anything from either of you."

"Honey, please, let me explain." He dropped the glass and went to the bed.

Sarah punched him, her small fists flying in the air, hitting him again and again. "Shut up! Shut up! Shut up!"

"Sarah, I'm sorry. I'm so sorry." His eyes leaked tears. "It was a mistake."

Sarah cried and screamed. She grabbed her sides and fell back on the bed, her body twitching. "I hate you."

Joe looked at Mallory. She smiled at him.

"How could you?" He sounded broken.

"I didn't think keeping the secret was fair to her."

"I should have let you die." Fury raged through him. He jumped off the bed, knocking Mallory to the floor. His hands wrapped around her neck. "I'm gonna kill you."

"What is all the commotion in here?" Richard assessed the situation. "Call 911," he yelled to Robert, then went to pull Joe off Mallory."

The ambulance bounced along University Ave. then turned into the emergency area of John Sealt's Hospital. They unloaded Sarah and rushed her into the ER.

"Her blood pressure is high and her heart rate is unsteady." The paramedic told the doctor on call. After getting Sarah settled and paperwork signed the ER doctor paged Dr. Burton.

Joe, Richard and Robert waited for more than an hour. The tension so strong it pulled tighter than a cable attached to the drill bit tunneling toward the center of earth. Joe sat silent. Richard kept giving Joe accusing glares.

When Richard went to get some coffee, Robert walked over to Joe. "Here." He handed Joe some crumpled papers.

Joe's hands shook as he looked at the pictures. "I never meant to hurt Sarah." Joe walked to the window, his bulky shoulders shaking. Robert came up behind him and just stood there.

"Why don't you hate me?" Joe asked through gritted teeth.

"I know my sister. Mallory is blackmailing me with pictures too."

"Now your dad has all the reason he needs to hate me."

"Dad had always admired you, although you have screwed up big time."

Dr. Burton entered with Richard, his face grim, his eyes serious and doubtful. Joe rushed toward him. "How is Sarah?"

"Not good, I'm afraid." He took his glasses off. "Her preeclampsia has developed into full blown eclampsia. She's having seizures which drastically reduce the oxygen to the baby. I'm giving her magnesium sulfate treatment to prevent premature delivery. But I have to be honest, if the seizures don't stop soon, I'll have to take the baby."

"But she's not far enough along," Joe said.

"It's going to be risky but we'll do everything we can for the baby."

"What are the odds of the baby surviving?"

"At twenty-eight weeks, not good." Dr. Burton slid his glasses on. "I'll do what I can." He left.

Tears filled Joe's dark eyes. He looked at his father-in-law. Richard's eyes were moist as well.

"I'm holding you personally responsible if anything happens to my daughter or grandchild." He walked over to the chair and sat down.

Forty minutes later Dr. Burton appeared in green scrubs. "Both Sarah and the baby are in stress. I have no choice but to do a C-section."

"Can I be there?" Joe asked.

"I'm sorry, but this is an emergency." He put a matching hat on. "I'll let you know how things go as soon as I can."

"More waiting," Joe sighed. "I'm going to get some coffee. Anyone want something?"

"No, I'm fine." Robert watched Joe leave. He sat down next to his father. "You could cut him some slack. That's his wife and daughter in there."

"They wouldn't be fighting for their lives if it weren't for him."

"We don't know the whole story."

"Cheating on your sister is bad enough, but with Mallory." He jerked up, out of the chair. "His wife's own sister, that's inconceivable."

"And you're not placing any blame on Mallory?"

"Yes!" Richard clenched his fists. "I blame her and Joe." He paced a few steps. "If anything happens to Sarah or the baby, I'll kill them both."

Joe was dressed in the same kind of green scrubs the doctor wore two hours earlier. After donning a hat, gloves and shoe covers, he went into the premature nursery. His little daughter lay under a large light that reminded him of hatching chicken eggs when he was a small boy. She didn't look much bigger than a chicken egg. If he could hold her, she'd fit in the palm of his hand.

He touched the glass and prayed that she'd be strong enough to make it. He noticed all the tubes coming out of her tiny body, making her look like she'd been caught in a spider's web. In a way she had.

Mallory's scheming and blackmailing had woven a web so tight that he couldn't move. When she moved in for the kill, he'd been helpless to stop her. He felt powerless to save his marriage or his baby.

"Dear God, take me, not my child." He'd give up his own life. Do whatever it took to make things right.

As he watched the infant's lips move slightly, he took comfort in the fact that she was still alive. He listened to the slow hum of the machinery and the uneven beeping of the heart monitor. There were more machines hooked up, keeping his daughter alive than it took to run an oil rig.

He stood there, staring at the naked, shriveled bundle that was a creation of him and Sarah. She looked so tiny. So helpless. He was just about to make a deal with God or the devil, which ever would save his daughter, when the beeping on the monitor got louder and closer together.

Suddenly there was a flurry of nurses and doctors, shouting orders and yelling out stats. Joe got pushed aside. Tears coursed down his cheeks as he listened to the dreaded words, "There's no heartbeat."

Chapter 10

Sarah lay on the hard mattress, tears leaking out of her eyes like a broken faucet. Her body hurt, her head ached and her heart felt crushed. She was an empty shell of the woman she used to be.

She'd had everything the world could offer. The innocent dreams of a little girl had been hers, for a while. Then, in the space of a few hours, everything had been taken away. Ripped away like the baby from her uterus. Her marriage was over, her daughter dead.

"Sarah, honey." Joe cautiously took a few steps inside the door.

"Go away." Her voice sounded weak. No malice or hatred as he'd expected, just hopelessness.

He continued to the bed. He wanted to hold her, cry in her arms. Grieve together. But he didn't want to push his luck. He stuffed his hands into his pockets to keep from touching her. He stood there not saying anything. What could he say?

Maybe she'd have some pity on him and make the first move. Say something, anything. But Sarah only stared blankly, her white face looking like a ghost. Dark circles formed under eyes and her lips were dried and cracked.

"Sarah, will you let me explain?" Joe finally said.

No answer.

"I never meant for any of this happen." He sat down in the chair placed by her bed. "I was drunk and we'd just had a big fight and I don't even remember how I ended up in Mallory's room." The excuses sounded weak, even to him. How did he expect Sarah to buy them? "I'm sorry, baby. I'm so sorry."

That word penetrated her heart. She looked at Joe. "Did you get to see our baby?"

"Yes," Joe whispered.

"Was she beautiful?"

"Yes." He wiped his eyes. "She looked just like you."

"I killed her."

"No." Joe scooted closer to the bed and took her hand. "It's not your fault."

"I tried to fight the contraction pains but they got too strong." Tears rolled down her cheeks. "My baby is dead."

"None of this is your fault." Joe squeezed her hand.

"No, it's Mallory's fault. Everything is Mallory's fault." Sarah stared off again.

Joe slammed the door of his motel room shut, threw his suit coat across the room and plopped down on the bed. He loosened his tie, wanting nothing more than to get out of this monkey suit.

The baby's funeral had been hard. Even though it was his child they buried, he felt like a stranger. Everyone rallied around Sarah and ignored him. Robert, Maria and Mrs. Santiago had been the only three people to even offer him any condolences.

Joe understood everyone's reaction, it was not like he didn't blame himself already, but would it have killed anyone to give him a hug and say, "I'm sorry for your loss." A little sympathy was all he wanted.

Joe stood and paced around the room. He'd decided not to go back to house. The service at the cemetery had been excruciating enough. Plus, he didn't think Richard would let him on the property. However, he did want to see Sarah. He'd wait until most of the people left then try to sneak in to see her.

His heart broke at the empty look she'd given him at the funeral. She'd walked up to the casket and laid a pink rose on top. When she looked up at him, her eyes held nothing. Not love or hate. Not condemnation or mercy. No light or darkness. Her expression had been blank, unfeeling, lost.

"What have I done?" His heart ached with regret. "How could I have been so stupid?" With his thoughts turning to Mallory, he felt the tension and anger boil to the surface. At least she'd had the decency to stay away from the burial. They may have been having another service if she'd shown up.

The sun turned the wide expanse of the sky into shades of pink, purple and orange, but the serenity of the sunset did nothing to ease the tension in Joe's heart. He punched in the code for the gate then ran along a side path leading to the house, hoping to avoid the cameras that watched the driveway.

He ducked behind some bushes when he heard a car coming down the drive. He recognized the white SUV as Mrs. Santiago's and figured she was running an errand. *Good, one less person to catch me*, he thought. Although, Mrs. Santiago would never rat him out.

After creeping around the side of the house he went up the front steps and carefully opened the door. All this work made him feel like James Bond, but he hadn't seen Sarah in two weeks. They'd decided to hold off on the burial until Sarah was strong enough to be there. The last time he'd talked to her was in the hospital room and he desperately wanted – no, needed – to see her. To hold her and cry with her.

After checking around the few rooms off the entryway and thinking the coast was clear, he started toward the stairs.

"Where do you think you're going?" Richard's deep voice stopped him.

"I'm going to see my wife." Joe turned to face the fiery eyes of his father-in-law.

"I don't think that's a wise idea."

"I just want to talk to her." Joe stepped closer. "She is still my wife."

"Not for long."

"What?" Joe went numb. *Surely she wouldn't divorce me without talking about it. We talk about everything.* He mentally shook his head. No, this was typical Richard trying to control everything. "I'll believe she has filed for a divorce when she tells me so with her own mouth." He squared his shoulders.

Richard took a few steps, closing the small gap between them. "You weaseled your way into this family by pretending to love my daughter, then you ripped out her heart and killed her child." Richard's face hardened and his voice rose with each accusation.

"I never pretended to love Sarah," Joe stared him down. "I did love her and I still do."

"How can you even say that?" His face softened a little. "You slept with her sister."

"There are two sides to the story, sir. Mallory is just as much to blame."

"You cheated on my daughter." Richard pointed at Joe's chest. "Who you cheated with and why is immaterial."

"I can't undo the past. I can only take responsibility for my mistakes and throw myself on Sarah's mercy. Maybe she'll be able to find forgiveness in her heart." He looked into Richard's light brown eyes, finding no mercy.

"Fat chance!" Richard walked to the door, opening it. "I'll see you in hell before I allow her to stay married to you."

Joe walked to the door. "She's a grown woman and you can't control her."

"I guess we'll wait and see who wins." Richard slammed the door shut behind Joe.

Sarah heard voices yelling and went to see what was going on. Joe had come. Part of her wanted to see him, but part of her couldn't handle it yet. She was thankful her dad had sent him away.

She felt thirsty and slowly made her way into the kitchen. Everyone would have a fit if they saw her walking. The cesarean hurt with each step but it felt good to be moving. Besides, the doctor had said to take it easy, not be confined to bed. However, her dad and the staff had seen to it that she wasn't allowed to move, and it kind of felt like being a prisoner.

Sarah walked into the kitchen and got out the orange juice. She went to the cupboard to get a glass. As she reached up a sharp pain gripped her abdomen. The glass slipped to the counter, rolling to a stop. She doubled over in pain.

The back door opened and Sarah looked over to see Mallory come in. She pulled her key out of the lock and looked surprised to see Sarah standing there.

"What are you doing in the kitchen?" Mallory asked.

"What are you doing in this house?" Sarah's harsh tone shocked Mallory.

"You don't own this house. Besides I'm still a part of the family." Mallory walked by, her expensive perfume almost choking Sarah.

"You'll have to talk with Dad about that."

"You'd just love it if he cut me out of the will, wouldn't you?" Mallory sneered. "Daddy's little princess would get everything."

"Whatever happens to you is your own making." Sarah fought the tears threatening to fall. She didn't want any emotions showing while she faced her enemy. Hadn't Dad always said that negotiations were better settled when you left your heart at the door?

"Of course, everything is my fault, as usual," Mallory huffed. "You don't get blamed for anything."

"What did I ever do to you, Mallory?" Sarah felt her knees shaking, her pulse racing and beads of sweat forming on her brow. "Why do you hate me so much?" Tears sprang to her eyes, no matter how hard she tried to stop them. "All my life you've treated me bad. But this?" Sarah touched her sore stomach. "You slept with my husband and killed my baby. What did I ever do to deserve this?" Tears streaked down her pale face. "Why?"

"Why?" Mallory's eyebrows shot up in surprise. "You took everything away from me from the minute you were born. You killed my mother. Then, you stole father's love and affection. He always doted on you and pushed me aside. I've hated you from the moment you came home from the hospital." Mallory crossed her arms. "As for Joseph? Well, I saw him first and you had to go and steal him away too. You deserve everything that's happened."

"Joe was never in love with you." Sarah felt anger rolling inside of her.

"He would have loved me if you hadn't batted those innocent eyes and played the *Oh, help me, I need a big strong man to save me*, part."

"You've twisted everything in that small brain of yours. Oh, wait, it isn't your brain that's too small, it's your heart." Sarah stood straighter. "You've never been anything but a whore and you've borne this family a bad name from the first married man you screwed at sixteen."

"My sexual history has nothing to do with you."

"It does when it involves my husband." Sarah had never felt so much hate before. "Wait a minute." Her hazel eyes lightened a green as the thought dawned on her. "I know why you showed me those awful pictures. Even after you got Joe in the sack, he still didn't want you, did he? He still chose me over you."

Mallory eyes narrowed. "Only because you went and got yourself pregnant. How could he leave with a baby on the way?"

"So you thought you'd eliminate the competition?"

"Not that you were much competition. It'd take a saint not to get bored with you."

"And the baby?"

"Just an innocent bystander." Mallory shrugged. "I have some things I need to get." She turned and started to walk away.

Sarah screamed and threw the glass at her head.

Joe went to a burger joint, but didn't feel like eating. He decided to drive around a bit and clear his head. He left the main roads of Galveston and took the long, winding routes through the plains.

The land was flat and fast. He pressed the accelerator down in his old pickup and watched the stars fly by in the open sky. He ended up at his favorite lake. He thought about Sarah. He'd brought her here on a date once.

Working on an oil rig is a hard and demanding job with crappy hours. Since he worked twelve hour shifts, sometimes it had been hard finding time to see her. So, they had planned some evening activities.

He drove her up here and they had a picnic under the stars. He'd turned his radio up and they listened to old tunes like: The Carpenters, Neil Diamond, Elvis and the Bee Gees. They stretched out on a blanket and tried to find as many constellations as they could. Since Joe only knew Orion by the three stars that made up his belt, Sarah had won.

"How do you know so much about the stars?" Joe asked.

"I don't know. I just love nature, I guess." She turned on her side to face him. "That's why I work so hard to protect the environment. If we keep ruining it the way we're doing, nothing will be left for our grand kids."

"But doesn't that put you at odds with your family? I mean they are in the oil business and it's one of the processes stripping our land."

"I do feel like an outcast sometimes, but Dad is always cool about my opposing opinions. He's always encouraged us to think for ourselves. Plus, he tries really hard to listen to my ideas and implement them."

"That must be nice." Joe tensed.

"It is, but I still miss my mom, even though I never knew her."

"Not knowing her, doesn't mean you won't miss her."

"I know. I just feel cheated sometimes. Robert and Mallory have memories of her and I don't." She rolled over on her back. "Do you think she can see me?"

"Of course." Joe pointed to a star. "You see that bright star way over there?"

"Yes."

"I'll bet that's your mom."

"What?" Sarah sat up.

"Sure." Joe smiled. "I bet she's walking around heaven and in the daytime she jumps on clouds to look down and see what you're doing. And when night comes she uses stars."

"How do you know it's that star?"

"It's the brightest one in the sky. It's not always the same star. She probably uses a different one each night, but it'll always be the brightest star because it's shining with her love."

"That's the sweetest thing anyone has ever said to me."

"Then why are you crying?" Joe looked perplexed.

Sarah shook her head, sending her honey colored hair tumbling around her shoulders. "I'm just happy, that's all." She cupped his face. "How did I get so lucky as to have you fall into my life?"

"Well, I didn't exactly fall, more like I bulldozed my way into your life." He leaned down and kissed her softly. "I'm working on drilling my way into your heart."

"You won't have to go too far." This time she kissed him with all the love she held in her heart.

As they merged closer together, their breathing became irregular, hearts beat faster and passion exploded. Joe laid her back, looking into her warm eyes. "I love you Sarah Dillingham." He kissed a trail down her neck and started to unbutton her shirt.

"No." Sarah sat up, passion still clinging in her eyes. "I love you too, Joe, but I want to wait until my wedding night."

Joe's hands stilled. The realization that she was a virgin dawned on him. "Then you'll wait for *our* wedding night because I intend to marry you."

"You're not mad?"

"To be honest, all the talk about your mom watching us from that star made me feel uneasy."

Sarah smiled. "When we get married, I want the ceremony outside and at night so mom can watch."

"I think we need to work on your dad first."

"Dad already likes you. He's already promoted you."

"But that's work." Joe kissed her. "You're his daughter. That's different."

"Well, I love you and you make me happy. Daddy will give me anything to make me happy."

Joe smiled at the memory. Sarah had gotten everything she wanted. They had eloped to Hawaii, combining the marriage and honeymoon in one package. Even though Richard had been furious at first, having reservations about her marrying a worker, especially with no prenup, he eventually gave his blessing. Then he paid for an outlandish wedding ceremony three months later, which had been more for the benefit of his reputation with friends and work acquaintances than for

Sarah. However, she did go along with the plans but insisted that the ceremony take place at night.

And now, Sarah sat alone in their bedroom, broken hearted and surrounded by grief. Their daughter lay buried in the ground. "All because of me."

He needed to see her, needed to try and explain things. Getting back in his truck he drove back to the house. Maybe the guards would be asleep and not notice him this time.

Joe made it around the corner of the house and went to the back door this time. He noticed that Mrs. Santiago's SUV was still gone. That seemed odd, but was fortunate for him as her bedroom was closest to the kitchen. She'd be the first one to hear him come in.

Using his key he unlocked the door and entered the kitchen. Closing the door, he stood there for a few minutes allowing his eyes to adjust to the darkness. What had he been thinking? He couldn't sneak around in the dark, he was bound to run into something, but he also couldn't risk someone seeing the light. Making his way through the kitchen he tripped over something on the floor and fell into the counter. "Damn!" He stood and felt his way over to the wall. Maybe no one would notice the kitchen light and he could search for a flashlight.

He flipped the switch then froze. Mallory lay sprawled out on the tile floor, a black knife sticking out of her chest. A pool of red surrounded her dark hair.

Joe covered his mouth so he wouldn't scream. Not wanting to get caught, he ran for the door. He grasped the knob.

Just then Mrs. Santiago came into the kitchen and screamed.

Chapter 11

The sirens blared through the old historic neighborhood, waking the occupants from their Victorian houses and alerting them that something was wrong. The Galveston police stopped in front of the stately, turn of the century brick structure that had been in the Dillingham family for generations.

The first two uniformed officers at the scene went into the kitchen and checked the victim for a pulse. The big, bulky guy looked at his slim, blond partner and shook his head. The woman officer then gathered the family members in the living room and started questioning them, while he called for a homicide investigating team to be dispatched. Two more first responders arrived on the scene and went to work taping off the yard and kitchen.

Other officers canvassed the neighbors to see if anyone had seen or heard anything. An hour later two detectives dressed in blue jeans and crumbled T-shirts arrived. Another car carried the impeccably dressed sergeant, Burt Wallace.

"Why do you two always look like bums?" The sergeant asked.

"Because you always call me when I'm asleep," Tom McCalahand grumbled.

"You know that most murders happen late at night or early in the morning, you should be used to the hours."

"Well, I'd appreciate a daytime killer," Tom said.

"Me too," Sam agreed.

"Maybe the next murderer will take your advice." Burt smiled. "He may even hang around so we can apprehend him without any work. And, just to make our job really easy, he'll confess."

"That works for me." Tom looked at Sam, who nodded his head in agreement.

"Let's go." Burt laughed. "This case isn't going to be easy."

They went into the kitchen and watched as the forensic team went to work dusting for prints, bagging evidence and taking pictures. The detectives talked with the first responders and took notes.

"The main suspect was caught leaving. He's in the living room with the family." The young officer pointed to the body. "Mallory Dillingham. The heiress of the Dillingham oil company."

"That's funny." Sergeant Burt Wallace looked at the bloody victim. "Mallory means unlucky."

"How do you always know the meanings of names?" Tom asked.

"I have five children and ten grandchildren. I've read more names and their meanings than Mr. Webster."

"Webster is a dictionary not a name book."

"Well, they have name dictionaries too," Burt defended.

Once they had all the information, the uniformed officers left. Burt sent Sam to finish questioning the neighbors and look around outside. Once the victim's body could be removed without contaminating or destroying any other evidence, he called the Medical Examiner's Office.

The coroner bent over the body making notes and taking off her jewelry and putting her personal things into a large envelope.

"What is the time of death?" Tom's tall, gangly body stood behind the short, plump coroner.

"Waiting on the thermometer," the coroner said.

"The main suspect was caught at eleven," Tom noted.

"The body is too stiff for TOD to be that recent." He moved Mallory's arm. "Rigor mortis sets in between two and six hours. She's still pretty flexible but starting to stiffen so I'm guessing she's been dead a few hours." Reaching over the abdomen, he pulled out the thermometer. "Body temp is 92.5 degrees. That puts TOD between seven and nine."

"I still like this guy for the murder," Tom said.

"Do you think he stabbed the victim then hung around for a couple of hours?" Burt asked.

"Stranger things have happened," Tom shrugged his thin shoulders. "Maybe he came back."

"So he could get caught?" Burt shook his graying head. "I don't think we're that lucky."

"Well she wasn't too lucky either."

"As I said, that is what her name means."

"I guess now her name means dead."

They watched as two guys loaded the body on a gurney.

"Hey, Burt, look here." The coroner pointed to something that had been under the body.

"Let's number and get a picture of this." Burt pointed to the forensic investigator holding a camera.

The coroner stood and handed a crumpled picture to the older detective.

"Looks like the victim with the suspect," Burt said.

"You mean the unlucky suspect." Tom smiled and wagged his blond eyebrows. "Maybe it is our lucky day after all."

"Let's go interview the family while the crew finishes up here," Burt said.

The two officers went into the family room where everyone had gathered.

"Mr. Dillingham, I'm sorry for your loss. I'm Sergeant Burt Wallace." They shook hands. "This is detective Tom McCalahand."

"Is all of the family and staff here?" Tom asked.

"Everyone except my daughter Sarah, she's in her room resting. I'm afraid with all the turmoil we had to give her a sedative." Richard looked tired. Lines and wrinkles deepened around his mouth and eyes making him look frail and old. "We just had a funeral for her baby earlier today. This situation was just too much for her."

"That's fine." Tom looked at Burt. "It makes our job quicker if we talk with everyone as soon as possible. There's no harm in waiting to speak with your daughter."

"Thank you," Richard sat on the couch, putting his arm around a sobbing Mrs. Santiago.

"Who found the victim?" Burt opened his notebook.

"I did."

"And who are you?"

"Reina Santiago," Richard said. "She's been the housekeeper for almost thirty-five years."

"What time did you find the body?"

"She screamed just before eleven. We called you right away." Richard tensed, not liking the line of questions.

"I know you're trying to protect your family, Mr. Dillingham, but we need her to answer the questions."

Richard nodded. "It's just that she's so upset." He hugged her.

"I'll be all right, sir." She gave a weak smile.

"I take it you knew the victim?" Tom asked.

"Ever since she was a baby." She held her hands apart to indicate a small baby.

"Did you hear any noise or commotion before you discovered the body?"

"No." She blew her nose. "But I took a sleeping pill and went to bed early. I'm afraid I was out like a stone."

"What time did you go to bed?" Burt wrote in his notebook.

"I'd say around seven or a little after. I left around six to do some errands."

"You were only gone for an hour?"

"About that." Mrs. Santiago nodded her head. "I got Sarah's prescription refilled then picked up the laundry from the cleaners."

"Did you go into the kitchen before you went to bed?"

"No. I went around to the service door. I brought Sarah her sedatives then went to my bedroom from the service hallway."

The line of questioning went on until they had a detailed account of where everyone had been and any sounds that they might have heard. Richard had been making some long distance phone calls. Maria had been out with a friend, then she'd done a few chores before going to bed. Robert had been at his campaign headquarters trying to focus his attention on the upcoming election. He'd come home around ten and gone to bed. That left Joe.

"What were you doing in the kitchen?" Tom asked.

"I wanted to see my wife," he said.

"He was caught sneaking in here earlier and I threw him out and told him not to come back." Richard stared hard at Joe.

"I didn't kill Mallory," Joe yelled. "I just wanted to talk with Sarah."

"Is there a reason you aren't staying here?" Burt asked.

Joe stayed silent.

"Does this picture have something to do with you and your wife's separation?" He held up the plastic bag containing the picture.

"Damn! Where'd you get that?" Joe tried to grab it.

Burt pulled it out of reach. "You can't touch the evidence."

"I know how this looks but I swear to you she was already dead when I got here." Joe ran an agitated hand through his hair.

"Do you have an alibi?"

"I went for a drive."

"By yourself?"

"Yes," Joe said. "I was at a lake with no one around for miles."

"No alibi and a strong motive. Things aren't looking good for you Mr. Barnes."

"But I don't have a motive. Mallory already showed Sarah the pictures of us. That's why I'm at a motel. That's why our baby is dead." Joe clenched his fists. "Mallory Dillingham was a vicious, evil slut. I'm glad she's dead. I didn't kill her, but I wish I would have been the one to do it."

"It's not a good idea to say things like that in front of police during a murder investigation." Tom took out his handcuffs. "I'm afraid you're under arrest."

The detectives started interviewing the office employees the next day. After talking with all the secretaries, business partners and stockholders, they got around to William Moss.

"How long have you worked for the Dillingham's?"

"Twenty years." He fidgeted with the knot of his tie.

"What made you go against Richard Dillingham in the takeover?" Burt asked.

"I ... umm ..." He coughed. "I thought Mallory had some innovated ideas."

"And the sexual affair had no bearing on your decision?" Tom stared at him.

"Wh ... What affair?" He stammered. Beads of sweat gathered on his forehead.

"Several people told us you and Mallory were having an affair." Burt tossed a file stuffed with papers on the table. "All of these employees, to be exact."

"They're lying." His chest puffed out indignantly.

"How do you explain the odd moans coming from her office when you were in there with her?" Tom asked.

William just stared at the folder and said nothing.

"Of course you weren't the only one having sex in her office." Burt looked at his notebook. "According to several secretaries the newly appointed vice president was heard screaming in pleasure several times."

William's balding head snapped up, his beady eyes hardened behind the wire rimmed glasses. "That's another lie."

"I don't know," Tom said. "Mallory Dillingham liked to have sex." He leaned closer, dropping his voice to a whisper. "Hot, heavy and very kinky sex."

"No she didn't," William shouted. "She wasn't like that at all."

"Really?" Burt looked at his notepad again. "We have witnesses that say she slept around a lot."

"She did whatever it took to get what she wanted," William admitted. "But she wasn't a slut."

"It sounds like you were in love with her."

"I've been in love with her for a long time."

"It must have hurt when she used you, then just dumped you like that," Tom said.

"Why don't you tell us what happened?" Burt suggested, his tone gentle, understanding.

William looked into his blue-gray eyes, finding a peace that he needed. "I was hurt and angry at her. She used me to help take over the company. I thought we were going to be partners. That she'd appoint me as VP and we'd run the company together."

"But she appointed someone else as VP," Tom said.

"I was furious." His meaty fists pounded the table. "She did promote me from accountant to chief financial officer, but she gave the VP position to that John Colthrop."

"How did you feel when you heard that they were having sex in her office?" Burt asked.

"Humiliated." He hung his head. "I actually heard them going at one time. I went to drop off some figures. You could hear the two of them throughout the whole building."

"What did you do?" Burt probed.

"I just left the folder with her secretary and told her to give it to Mallory when she wasn't busy."

"That sounds like a good motive for murder," Tom said.

"I didn't kill her," William protested.

"Do you have an alibi?"

"No, I was home alone." William stood. "I may have hated her for using me the way she did, but I didn't kill her."

"Don't plan any trips out of the state," Burt said.

The guards brought Joe into a small room. A man dressed in a suit sat at the square table. He stood when the door opened. "I'm Dave Tellbit from the office of Sandburgh and Stanly."

"Isn't that the firm that represents Richard Dillingham?" Joe shook his hand then sat down.

"Yes, your wife asked me to help you."

"Does Richard know?"

"I'm sure he does by now." He smiled.

"He's going to be furious."

"That's why the office sent me. Mr. Sandburgh and Mr. Stanly wouldn't dare cross Mr. Dillingham, but they wanted to help your wife."

"Thank you."

"You're bail hearing is coming up and we need to focus on getting you out of here."

"That would be wonderful."

Joe stood beside his lawyer during the whole process of getting bail set.

"We want the defendant held without bail." the DA looked at the judge. "He's a flight risk and due to the violent nature of this crime we feel he's a threat to the community."

"That's nonsense," Dave argued. "My client has no money therefore isn't a flight risk."

"He's married to money." The DA pointed out.

"That's not the point," Dave argued.

"Enough," The judge ordered. "This is a bail hearing not the trail."

"Your Honor, my client is accused of killing one of the members of the family in which he married into. I don't think they will help him flee."

"Then how is he affording to pay you?"

"That's not the issue."

"Will you two stop fighting and get to the point." The judge banged his gavel.

"The people ask you to set the bond at one million dollars."

"That's crazy," Dave said. "My client can't afford that. We ask that it be lowered to three hundred thousand."

"The defendant already has a criminal record," The DA said.

"That has no bearing on the bail," Dave said. "You shouldn't even be bringing it up right now."

The Judge set the amount at five hundred thousand dollars.

"I can't afford that," Joe said.

"Don't worry. I have arrangements for your bail."

Joe caught sight of Sarah sitting in the back of the room. His heart stopped. She'd not only paid for his defense and bail but she came to the hearing. Should he dare think that maybe she'd forgiven him?

She met his eyes then stood and walked out of the room. He went after her, fighting the throng of people crowding the hallway. "Sarah, wait." He caught up to her.

She stopped.

"Thanks for getting me out of jail."

"You may be a cheater and a liar but you're not a killer."

"Can we go somewhere and talk?"

"No."

Joe searched those brownish green eyes eyes for some sign of forgiveness but found none. "I'm truly sorry, Sarah."

"Stop." She held up her small hand. "I don't want to hear it. I don't believe you killed Mallory, but I can't forgive you."

Maybe if he gave her a little more time she'd come around. However, time seemed to be running out on him. "I never meant to hurt you."

"Goodbye, Joe." Sarah walked down the hallway.

Chapter 12

"Mr. Dillingham, thank you for coming in." Burt shook his hand.

"It didn't sound like I had much of a choice." Richard sat at the table. "Should I call my lawyer?"

"You're not under arrest," Tom clarified. "We only want to ask some questions."

"We recently found out that Mallory took control of Dillingham Oil," Burt said.

"Yes, that's true, but I was preparing a case for court to gain back control."

"Were you angry that your own daughter would deceive you like that?" Tom asked.

"Hell, yeah, I was angry," Richard yelled. "But I didn't need to kill her. I would have won in court."

"I have three daughters, Mr. Dillingham. I know how much time and emotional investment goes into raising them," Burt said. "You change their diapers, teach them to walk and talk, tuck them in at night, buy their cars, pay for their schooling and give them the best of everything. It must be devastating to have her pay you back by stabbing you in the back."

"Is that why she moved out recently?" Tom asked.

"I did ask her to move out, but not for the reason you think," Richard defended. "I was trying to protect Sarah."

"Mallory and Sarah didn't get along?" Burt asked.

"Mallory liked pushing Sarah's buttons. She did ever since they were children." He shook his head. "When Sarah became pregnant, Mallory kept making insults and provoking her. I didn't want Sarah under any more stress, so I asked Mallory to leave."

"Did you know about the affair between Joe and Mallory?"

"No. Or I'd have kicked Joe out with Mallory. I only found out the same night Sarah did."

"Do you think the affair was the reason for Sarah losing her baby?" Burt asked.

"I know it was the reason. Sarah had already been having complications and was told to rest. After seeing those pictures, she went into seizures." Richard's eyes misted. "Why are you asking all these questions? You already have Joe in custody."

"We're just trying to see the whole picture," Tom said.

"You're alibi isn't exactly sound proof," Burt added. "You were alone with no one to verify your whereabouts."

"You think I killed my daughter?" Richard stood up. "That's preposterous."

"You had time and motive."

"Joe did it!" Richard said. "He was caught leaving the scene."

"The evidence is strong against him, but the fact of the matter is she took your company away and killed your grandchild." Tom leaned forward on the table. "That's a strong motive."

"Joe killed my grandchild," Richard corrected them. "I'm not saying another word until I have a lawyer."

"That won't be necessary at this point and time." Burt walked to the door, opening it. "You're free to go."

As the day wore on, the two detectives interviewed more workers from the office then turned to the oil rig. After talking with the derrickman and three roughnecks, who all praised Joe's work and moral ethics, the last worker came in and took a seat. He ran a hand through his spiked brown hair then cursed as he messed up his hairdo.

"Give us your name and spell it, please." Burt turned on the tape recorder.

"Michael Garcia but everyone calls me Snickers."

"Why?" Tom asked.

"Because I eat a lot of candy bars."

"Oh," Tom tried not to laugh. "So how long have you worked for the Dillingham company?"

"Just a couple of months."

"What do you think of Joe Barnes?"

"He's a good boss."

"Wasn't Mallory Dillingham your boss?"

"Well, technically, but I work with Joe."

"What did you think of Mallory?" Burt asked.

"I never talked with her. I only saw her from a distance, but she was hot."

"Did she come out to the site a lot?"

"Yeah, but it made Joe mad."

"Why?" Tom asked.

"I don't know but he always tensed up and yelled a lot when she came around."

"Maybe he didn't like having his boss breathing down his neck," Burt said.

"I don't think that was it, something else was going on between the two of them." Snickers fidgeted in his chair. "She was always standing real close and rubbing against him."

"What did Joe do?"

"Usually nothing, but on the last visit he pushed her down."

"Really?" Tom looked at Burt. "Did you ever overhear any of their conversation?"

"No. The rig is loud and I have to concentrate on my job."

"What happened after Mallory was pushed down?"

"Joe started up the steps, Ms. Dillingham got up from the ground and started after him, she followed him into his office."

"And?" Burt probed.

"I made a comment to Mickey that the boss was probably getting a little something from her."

"Did Mickey agree?" Tom flipped through his notes and noted that he was the derrickman.

"He said I was just a worm and didn't know what I was talking about. He said Joe was married to her sister, Sarah, and would never cheat on his wife, especially with someone like Mallory."

"What is a worm?" Burt interrupted.

"The new guy, sort of like a rookie."

"Um, okay," Burt said. "Do you know what Mickey meant by especially like Mallory?"

Snickers shrugged his wide shoulders. "No. But he went into the office a few minutes later and come out looking upset."

"Do you know what upset him?"

"Not for sure, but I figured it had something to do with the pipe being stuck. Maybe Joe yelled at him."

"Did you ask Mickey what happened?"

"I didn't think about it. In all the commotion I forgot until now."

"Commotion?" Burt raised a gray brow.

"Yeah, after Joe and Ms. Dillingham came out to fix the problem, there was an accident. A pipe slipped overhead and almost landed on Ms. Dillingham. She rolled out of the way and rolled off the side of the platform. She grabbed hold and was dangling there. Joe started to go forward then stopped and stared at her. I didn't think he was going to save her at first, but he finally did pull her up. She gave him a funny look and left a short time later."

"Do you remember when this happened?" Tom smirked at Burt.

"A few weeks ago."

"Thanks for coming in, Snickers."

After he left Tom and Burt looked through their notes. "Out of all the people we've interviewed, no one else mentioned that incident," Tom said.

"He could be making up the story," Burt pointed out.

"Why? He has nothing to gain and he hasn't worked as long as the others so his loyalty is weak."

"The first thing we need to do is get Mickey in here and find out what he saw in that office."

"Why don't we get a search warrant for the victim's apartment and the Dillingham house too," Tom suggested.

"Technically we don't need a warrant for the victim's apartment, only the house," Burt corrected.

"Smart ass," Tom laughed. "You know what I meant."

The detectives started interviewing the staff from the house. After talking with a calmer Mrs. Santiago, they called in Maria.

"Can you state your name and spell it, please?" Tom turned on the recorder for the umpteenth time that day.

"Maria Santiago." She leaned forward and spoke slowly.

Tom held back a laugh. "How long have you worked for the Dillinghams?"

"I started working in the house about five years ago, right after I finished college, but I've grown up in the house. My mother and I moved in after my dad left. I was just a girl."

"If you have a degree, why are you working as a maid?" Burt asked.

"My mom is getting older and I wanted to be around to help her." She couldn't tell them that she wanted to be around Robert. "I only went to college for my mom. I hated it."

"So, you've known the victim for a long time?"

"Yes, most of my life." She tensed and scratched her wrist.

"Were the two of you close?" Tom asked.

"No one was close to Mallory. She only thought about herself." Maria tucked behind her ear a few loose strands of hair that fell out of her pony tail.

"Sounds like there was bad blood between you two."

"Mallory Dillingham brought out the worst in everybody." She scratched the back of her hand.

"Was the blood bad enough to kill her?" Burt asked.

"What?" She stood with an explosion of Spanish.

"Sit down, Ms. Santiago." Burt stood, ready to subdue her if need be. "We are only trying to find the murderer."

"It's not me." She sat back down. "I already told you I was out with a friend."

"We need the friend's name," Tom said.

"Why?"

"To verify you're telling the truth."

"I don't lie." She crossed her arms under her chest, her silver bracelets jingling.

"What's wrong with your hand?" Burt noticed the red blotches covering it.

"I'm very sensitive to rubber gloves. I usually use synthetic gloves but we ran out of them and I used the regular ones." She scratched again. "It should clear up in a few days."

"Is there a particular reason you hated Mallory?" Tom asked.

"She was a selfish bitch." Maria's dark eyes hardened. "If that statement makes me a suspect then so be it, but it's the truth."

"I never said you were a suspect." Burt leaned forward. "However, the fact that you won't give us your friend's name is a little suspicious."

"I'm not at liberty to disclose it right now."

"That'll be all for now, Ms. Santiago, Thank you for coming in."

"Hey, you guys need to see this." The officer walked Burt and Tom to an office with a TV set. "We found this in Mallory's apartment." He pushed a button and the vivid images of Joe and Mallory having sex appeared on the screen.

Tom whistled. Burt looked away. The other officers laughed and joked.

"She must have made the still pictures off this video," Tom said.

"Why didn't Joe mention the video when we talked with him? He said Mallory was blackmailing him, but I thought she only had photos." Burt crinkled his forehead. "He's keeping something back."

"Probably because he's guilty," Tom said. "No jury would think he didn't kill her after viewing this."

"He looks drunk," Burt noticed.

"Yeah." One of the other officers agreed. "The best part is coming up."

"How many times have you watched this?" Burt raised a brow.

"I don't know, three or four." The guys laughed.

"According to Joe she used the pictures to blackmail him into getting Sarah to sign her shares over to Mallory." Burt was lost in thought, the wheels turning, trying to piece together the evidence.

"Joe also said that he forged his wife's signature and that gave Mallory the power to take the company away from her dad. But Mallory still told Sarah about the affair anyway," Tom stated.

"Exactly." Burt rubbed his chin. "If she already got what she wanted then why expose the affair?"

"Especially when she knew Sarah was having trouble with her pregnancy?" Tom noted.

"Do you think Mallory told her so she would lose the baby?" Burt's eyes brightened. "Maybe she didn't get what she wanted after all."

"She got the company, what else did she want?" Tom stared at the TV.

"Maybe she wanted Joe." Burt looked at the screen. "Maybe this whole set up wasn't only for the company. It might have been more personal."

"I don't know." Tom shook his head. "I mean, she seduces Joe and then sleeps with the accountant, who's helping her with the takeover. She sounds like a woman on a mission."

"But she dumped William Moss after the take-over." Burt pointed out.

"Can you blame her?" Tom asked.

"Why did she keep bothering Joe?"

"Snickers did say Mallory would stand too close and sometimes rub against him like a cat," Tom said.

"Why is it you can never remember names but when it comes to a nickname like Snickers, you remember that?"

"I don't know, I like Snickers."

"What do you make of a woman who steals the company away from her father, seduces and blackmails her brother-in-law, then destroys her sister's marriage and causes the death of her unborn baby?" Burt counted on his fingers. "Do you think she didn't have enough love growing up?"

"I think the young maid was right, Mallory Dillingham was a selfish bitch."

Mickey sat in the interview room, looking scared while the detectives grilled him.

"Snickers told us an interesting story when he was in here yesterday," Burt said. "He told us that Malory and Joe had a fight the last time she came out to the site."

"He also said that she almost got killed by a falling pipe," Tom added.

"Why didn't you say anything about this when we first talked with you?" Burt asked.

"I forgot about it." He shrugged. "It wasn't a big deal, she didn't die. Joe saved her."

"That's something else. He told us Joe hesitated before he pulled her up, as if he might let her fall."

"Joe would never do that."

"Well, Snickers also said that you didn't believe Joe would ever cheat on his wife especially with someone like Mallory," Burt said.

"It's true," Mickey defended.

"We know for a fact that they were having an affair," Tom said. "What do you think of that?"

Mickey's eyes widened but he didn't say anything.

"Don't look so shocked," Burt added. "You saw the two of them together."

"I never did."

"You didn't walk in on them in the office?" Tom asked.

Mickey thought. "Yes, but..."

"What did you see?" Burt fired the questions.

"Mallory had Joe pinned against the wall."

"Really?" Tom arched his brown brows.

"But it wasn't like that."

"Then how was it?" Tom asked.

"Joe told me she pushed him off balance and pounced on him just as I entered."

"And you believed him?" Burt asked.

"Yes. I know how Mallory can be." He looked down at the floor. "Or how she was."

"How was that?"

"She was a slut!" Mickey said, agitated. "She went after anything that moved."

"You know this from personal experience?"

"Yeah," he said softly. "We had a thing for a while."

"When?"

"A few years ago."

"What happened?"

"She got tired and moved on. With Mallory it was the thrill of the chase, once she caught you she got bored."

"Did it end badly?"

"Sort of. I knew how she was before hooking up so I just didn't let myself get too close. But, it still hurt when she dumped me."

"Were you hurt enough to kill her?"

"No."

"Do you think Joe finished the job?"

"No."

"Mallory blackmailed him then destroyed his marriage," Burt said. "And to top it all off when she showed Sarah the picture of them, Sarah went into seizures and the baby died. Don't you think Joe would be angry enough to kill after all that?"

Mickey didn't say anything.

"Are you protecting him?" Tom asked.

"No."

"Maybe you're protecting your job," Tom said.

"I'm not protecting anyone." Mickey stood. "I didn't kill her and neither did Joe."

Richard stared out the window in his study. The full moon hung in the navy sky like a spotlight, its illumination shedding a faint light across the path to the garden. Three days had ended since he'd found his daughter's bloodied body on the kitchen floor.

He'd yet to feel any emotion. Was it normal to have a child killed and not feel anything? He drank some more of his scotch. The amber liquid burned a path down his throat. Maybe the alcohol blocked the feelings of sadness he should be feeling. Maybe he just didn't care. After all, Mallory left a path of destruction in this life. Would she get her just reward in the afterlife?

"Dad." Sarah knocked on the open the door.

"Princess." Richard turned from the window, opening his arms wide.

Sarah went to him, embracing him fiercely. Tears slipped down her sunken cheeks. "I didn't know if you were still talking to me."

"Why wouldn't I?" He wiped a few tears away. "You're my daughter."

"I figured you'd be mad about Joe." She felt his body stiffen but his smile never wavered.

"I don't understand why you paid his bail?"

"I know he didn't kill Mallory." She looked into her father's loving eyes. "I know you're angry at him, so am I, but Joe's not a murder."

"I wish my faith was a strong as yours. The fact is I don't care if he did it or not. He belongs locked away after what he did to you."

She laid her head against his chest. "I can't let an innocent man go to prison. Even if I do wish he'd burn in hell along with Mallory."

"You're a better person than I am." He kissed the top of her head.

"Are you mad that I hired an attorney?"

"I already gave the company a good chewing out. But, I know how hard it is to say no to you."

"Then, you forgive me?"

"There's nothing to forgive. You must do what you think is right. I'll do what I think is best for this family."

"That could put us on opposite sides."

"Probably." Richard looked up at the moon. "But, we've been there before."

Sarah looked at the moon also. "Do you think mom is watching us right now?"

"I hope not," Richard sighed. "She'd be heart-broken to watch us struggle with all this grief."

"Do you think I caused this?"

Richard jerked away. Taking Sarah's shoulders and holding her at arms' length. "What would make you say that?" He demanded.

"If I hadn't been born, mom wouldn't have died."

"Oh, honey." Richard pulled her close. "When you found out you were pregnant, what did you feel?"

"Excitement, joy and a little scared."

"Your mother felt the same way. She would have done anything to keep you safe, including risking her life. The decision was never yours, or even mine to make. It belonged to your mother and she chose to give you life."

"I feel like I'm cursed," Sarah sobbed. "First mom dies giving birth to me then my baby dies. Why can't I do anything right?"

"Honey, it's not your fault. The circumstances were beyond your control." His eyes narrowed under his bushy brows. "If Joe and Mallory hadn't cheated behind your back, none of this would have happened."

"That's one more thing." She sniffled. "He wouldn't have cheated if I'd been a better wife. My marriage is falling apart and my baby is dead. Mallory has been murdered and I'm in the center of it all."

Richard held her while she cried. "We are all in the middle of this crisis. Let's just hope the storm passes soon." He untied the green handkerchief around his neck and handed it to Sarah. "Dry those tears and no more sympathy bashes. I believe people get what they deserve." He looked up at the moon. "Mallory got her payment and Joseph Barnes is next." He looked down at Sarah, her eyes red and swollen. He'd make Joe pay if it took every cent he owned. "You, my dear, are bound to reap the harvest of happiness. A good soul like yours can't stay down for long."

"Thanks, Dad." She blew her nose. "I just don't feel very blessed right now." She looked up at the moon, thinking about her mother. "Do you think Mom is holding my little girl right now?"

"Indeed, I do. That's why the moon is so bright."

"Maybe it was better my baby died. Now, Mom has a grandchild to spoil."

"Good point." Richard smiled, slightly.

"But, I'd still give anything to have them both here with me."

"Me, too, Princess. Me, too."

Chapter 13

Burt stood beside the coroner looking at Mallory's naked, cold body. The whiteness of her skin contrasted her black hair. A bruise had developed around the knife entry.

"She was stabbed three times." The coroner pointed to the shoulder. "One entry hit above the heart, lodging into the collar bone. The other two wounds went right into the heart, killing her." The short, pudgy coroner pulled the sheet down further to examine the wounds. "The angle of the blade is different with this wound." He pointed to the wound by the collarbone. "It went in straight as if the killer were standing even with the victim." He moved his finger down an inch. "These two wounds are at an angle suggesting the victim was on the floor when the blade entered her body, or the killer was much taller than she was."

"So, the killer could have stabbed her while she was standing. Then, after the victim fell on the floor, the killer stood over her and plunged the knife in two more times," Burt said. "Does it look like a crime of passion?"

"Possible." He pointed to the slice. "See this bruise isn't very dark." His hand moved to the second cuts. "These wounds, however, are bruised a lot, meaning the blade was thrust in with more force."

"So, the killer stabbed her once and when she didn't die, he stabbed her two more times with more force?" Burt wrote in his notebook.

"I guess the killer wanted to get the job done."

"What about the head wound?" Burt asked.

"There's a cut probably made by a small, heavy object that shattered on contact." He took a glass dish off the counter and showed Burt. "I got tiny glass fragments from her hair."

"There was a broken glass at the scene."

"The wound is consistent with a drinking glass. I'll send this out to compare the shards with a glass from the house."

"Any sign of rape?"

"No. I swabbed and found traces of semen but the sex looked consensual."

"Well, the list of sexual activity is beginning to look quite long."

"I suggest you get moving and find me samples to compare."

"Yes, sir." Burt saluted.

Tom visited the crime scene lab and took notes.

"Look at the blood splatter," the technician pointed to the pictures that she'd enlarged. "See these large spots between the droplets?"

"Yes."

"That tells me there was something on the floor when she got stabbed and it was removed after the killing."

"Like what?" Tom asked.

"Something small, maybe several pieces of something. The blood splatter indicates several large areas that are clean when there should be splatter."

"Any fingerprints?"

"One set. A partial and it was smudged a little, as if someone wiped off the knife but missed a spot."

"Whose is it?" Tom looked up from his notebook.

"Sarah Barnes."

Tom's brows rose in surprise.

"But she lives in the house and she could have used the weapon before the murder." The crime scene investigator explained.

"But if she tried to wipe it off that shows intent."

"Perhaps." Her blond brows rose to show doubt. "I also found some red, cotton threads caught in the handle. Traces of dirt and petroleum were on the handle, along with palm oil, lactic acid and xanthan gum."

"That sounds like one dirty knife," Tom commented. "What does all that junk tell you about the murder?"

"Well, it sounds like cleaning chemicals. If you get samples from the house I should be able to compare and see what fits the chemicals on the handle. But for now everything is guesswork." She crossed her arms. "Petroleum can be in some cleaners. Since the knife came from the kitchen, it could have been cleaned with these ingredients."

"If it had been cleaned, then why were there fingerprints on the handle?"

"Finding an answer to that is your job." She pointed at him. "I'm only telling you what I found at the scene."

"What about the broken glass?"

"Again, only one set of prints belonging to Sarah Barnes."

"Interesting." Tom made notes. "Thanks." He closed his notebook. "Let me know if anything else comes up."

"No problem."

Sarah dressed in a simple black dress. It was the second time within a week and a half that she attended a funeral. Her heart felt heavy, ready to break. Although she felt sad, no tears fell for her sister, pain and anger blocked them.

She'd helped her dad make all the arrangements, but nothing had prepared her for the emptiness she felt in her heart. Colorful flowers, soft music and kind words couldn't hide the relief. Her sister had been murdered, cut down like a common whore. Shouldn't she feel more than gratitude?

She felt sorry for her dad, and for Robert and for anyone else who would truly miss Mallory, but as far as she was concerned, someone had done her a huge favor. She thought about the pictures Mallory had shown her. She remembered the chaos in the delivery room and burying her daughter more than a week ago.

No one could ever convince her that life wouldn't be better with Mallory out of the way.

Richard stood by the casket, staring at his daughter's body. Mixed emotions churned in his stomach. She looked so beautiful, even angelic. Her ebony hair had been combed and floated around her shoulders, the dark contrast to her light skin, which now looked whiter than the satin lining the coffin.

How could someone look so innocent and be so deceiving? Why had she turned so evil? He couldn't keep the guilt and failure away. No matter how many times people told him he wasn't to blame, he didn't believe it. Could a child be born so full of hate? Had he been responsible for the choices she made? In trying to protect one child had he destroyed the other?

"Dad." Robert walked in dressed in a black three piece suit, looking like the debonair politician he was about to become. "How are you holding up?" He hugged Richard.

"Fine." He clung to his son. He'd never been a man to show emotion but he needed his family now. Too much grief had taken hold of his heart to care about appearances. "I just can't believe she's gone."

"I know." Robert looked at his sister. She'd gotten what she deserved but he still felt bad about the way she died. "She was so young. Do you think she could have changed if she'd lived longer?"

"I'd like to hope so." However there always hung the possibility that she could have grown more ruthless. The love of power and money had a way of doing that.

"Richard. Robert." Joe walked over to the casket. "I don't want to cause any trouble I only wanted to offer my condolence."

"How dare you!" Richard's face reddened. "You killed her."

"No, sir, I didn't."

"How dare you show your face here." Richard's hard stance weakened and his voice cracked. "This is all your fault."

"I take full responsibility for the affair and for forging Sarah's name, but I didn't kill Mallory."

"You killed my granddaughter, too," he said.

"Why do you seem to forget that she was my child?" Joe pointed to his chest. "My flesh and blood."

"If you had cared about anyone else besides yourself, she wouldn't have been born premature."

"There's no guarantee of that," Joe said.

"You've done enough damage. Get out!" Richard yelled.

"I admit my mistakes, but you can't place all of the blame on me. Mallory brought this on herself. I'm sorry for your loss. I truly am, however I'm not sorry she's dead."

"Get out!" Richard clutched his chest and started to crumble to the floor.

"Please go," Robert begged. "He can't take much more stress."

"I'm sorry." Joe walked away while Robert helped his dad to a chair. He looked back to make sure Richard was okay. He noted the color coming back into his cheeks and his breathing returned to normal.

He started to go out the door when he spotted Sarah coming in. He held open the door for her. She stopped, looked at him then continued through the door. Joe followed her back in.

"What are you doing here?" She asked.

"I wanted to offer my condolence."

"Are you sorry she's dead?" Sarah looked hurt. "Now you'll have to find some other bimbo to have dirty sex with."

"I don't want anyone else."

"Were you in love with her?" She clenched her teeth to keep the tears from falling.

"Never!" Joe stepped closer. "I never loved her and I never would have."

"You just used her for sex?"

"It wasn't like that." Joe ran his hand through his long, tangled hair. "I hated her and I'm not sorry she's dead. I know that makes me sound hard, mean and unkind. I know she was your sister but she ruined my life." He stepped closer. "She destroyed us." He stood, towering over Sarah. "I've never loved anyone the way I love you. I would have done anything to keep you."

"Even murder?"

"If you think I killed her then why did you post bail?"

"I don't believe you killed her." Sarah looked up into his eyes. She felt his vitality emitting like a fire. She wanted to press against him, soaking up his strength. "But I also don't believe you love me."

"What can I do to prove my love for you?"

"Nothing." With every ounce of strength she could muster, she walked away.

The ceremony had been simple and short. Robert delivered the eulogy, telling of the few times they had fun as children. However, most of his childhood had been spent being bullied by Mallory. As an adult he'd been blackmailed in one way or another. It had been hard coming up with the couple stories he told, no way could he have made a long, endearing speech about her good qualities. He was a politician, after all, not an actor.

The attendance turned out to be much larger than the family had expected. Most people had come for the family not because they cared about Mallory. In the past week, more and more friends had stopped by to offer their sympathy and to spill the stories of blackmail, threats, lies and dishonesty that Mallory had reveled in.

She'd gained control through sex and blackmail. Richard just couldn't figure out why running Dillingham Oil had been so important to her. Why had she gone through all the trouble when she would have inherited the company one day? Nothing about Mallory made any sense.

Joe sat at the bar, nursing a beer. The loud country music did little to ease the tension in his body. He felt like starting a fight just to relieve some of the pressure. When Tom and Burt came in and sat beside him, the tension pulled every nerve taut.

"Hey, can we buy you a drink?" Tom sat down.

"No, thanks. I have one." Joe held up his bottle. "Are you going to arrest me for drinking."

"Not unless you're under age." Burt smiled. "And I'm positive you're old enough to drink."

"Then what are you doing here?"

"We just wanted to have another little chat." Tom shrugged. "Thought this would be a friendlier place than hauling you back down to the station."

"What if I don't feel like chatting?" Joe drank his beer then set it down. "It's been a long, tough day."

"And you think getting drunk is going to help?" Burt quirked a gray brow.

"It beats thinking about what a hellhole my life has turned into."

"We saw the video of you and Mallory," Burt said. "Looks like drinking is what got you into this mess."

Joe paused, beer in midair. "You found the video?"

"Yeah," Tom said. "Some pretty racy stuff. Do you want to tell us the truth about the blackmail this time?"

"This is your last chance to come clean," Burt noted.

"What makes you think I lied?" He took a swig. "You can check the name on the letter."

"We did," Tom said. "And it is a forgery."

"I told you I forged the signature." Joe sipped his beer. "So why are you still bothering me?"

"Because we found out a few things that don't add up." Burt watched Joe's face for his reaction. "Like the fact that even after Ms. Dillingham stole control of the company, she still hung around you, like she was in love with you or something."

Joe tensed but didn't say a word.

"We have some eye witnesses that say she liked to stand very close to you on the jobsite," Tom said. "One guy said he saw the two of you making out in your office a few weeks before she died."

"That's a lie!" Joe burst. "She tripped me and I fell against the wall then she jumped on me before I could push her off."

"So the relationship wasn't over?"

"It was on my part," Joe sighed. "I would never have been with Mallory in the first place if it weren't for her blackmailing me."

"You wanted the relationship to end and she didn't?" Tom asked.

"I don't know what the bitch wanted." Joe's eyes hardened to stone. "I just wanted her out of our lives."

"Looks like you got your wish," Tom commented.

Joe stared at him.

"Why don't you tell us the truth about the black-mail?" Burt suggested.

"She got me on videotape and threatened to expose the whole thing if I didn't keep sleeping with her." Joe drank down the rest of his beer then motioned for another one.

"So she was blackmailing you into having sex with her?" Tom seemed surprised.

"Why didn't you just tell your wife?" Burt asked. "Seems like it would have been easier."

"I planned on telling her the truth after the first time. I knew I couldn't live with a secret that big, but before I could tell Sarah the truth, she told me about the baby." Joe drank from the new bottle placed in front of him. "I couldn't tell her after that. I had to protect both her and the baby."

"Sleeping with your wife's gorgeous sister is a great way of protecting her," Tom sneered.

"Shut up!" Joe slammed his beer down. "If I'd wanted Mallory, I would have married her."

"Sounds like she wanted you," Burt observed.

"She was never going to get me."

"Why did you choose Sarah over Mallory?" Tom asked.

"Because she is sweet and caring. She's everything good in my life." Joe fought back his emotions.

"The Dillingham money had nothing to do with it?" Tom asked.

"No." Joe stared him. "I could have had the money with Mallory."

"Then would you have slept with Sarah on the side?" Tom asked.

Joe grabbed the front of his shirt and pulled his right fist back.

Burt grabbed his arm. "Wait a minute," he cautioned. "Do you really want to go back to jail for assaulting an officer?"

Joe hesitated then pushed Tom away.

"Quite a temper you have." Tom straightened out his shirt. "Is that what happened to Mallory? You got mad and stabbed her."

"I told you I didn't kill her."

"Wasn't that the only way for her to stop black-mailing you into having sex?"

"No. That's why I forged the signature. She said we could quit having sex if I got Sarah on her side."

"When you couldn't talk Sarah into signing the papers, you forged her name," Burt said.

"Yes."

"Did Ms. Dillingham hold up to her side of the deal?" Tom asked.

"We didn't have sex again," Joe said. "But she did keep trying to talk me into it."

"Is that why you almost let her fall off the rig when the pipe fell?"

"I didn't let her fall, I pulled her up." Joe took a long drink. "Worst mistake of my life."

"So, if you had it to do over again, you'd let her fall?"

"Damn straight."

Tom looked at Burt. "When you pulled her up, did she say anything to you?"

"No. She gave me an angry look, though."

"Why?" Burt asked.

"Not sure, probably because she knew I wanted her gone. She knew that it was finally over between us."

"All that from one look?" Tom made a notation in his notebook. "Must have been one heck of a look."

"It was as cold as ice in Alaska." Joe threw some money on the bar. "It's been fun, but I should go." He walked away.

"What do you think?" Tom asked.

"I think he's telling the truth." Burt ordered a drink. "She got him drunk, seduced him, videotaped the whole thing then blackmailed him."

"When none of that worked to get Joe away from her sister, she exposed the affair."

"Yep." Burt sipped his gin and tonic. "Killing an innocent baby in the process."

"All of that proves motive enough for Joe to kill her. He has one heck of a temper." Tom's hand went up his chest, rubbing where Joe had grabbed him.

"You were being an ass," Burt said.

"Well, we can't both be the good cop." Tom watched the barmaid clear away the empty bottles. "What do you make of this whole situation?"

"I think Joe was caught between a rattlesnake and a viper."

"That's only because you want to be right."

"I am right." Burt smiled. "My gut is telling me he's not the killer."

"But the evidence says he is."

"Maybe not." Burt looked at Tom. "All the motives we have against Joe could apply to someone else."

"Who?"

"Someone who has even more motivation than Joe."

"Who?" Tom's loud tone said his patience was wearing out.

"Sarah Barnes."

Tom almost choked on his drink.

"Think about it," Burt said. "Sarah had just found out that her husband was cheating and lost her baby. The picture under Mallory's body is more than likely the same one she showed Sarah weeks earlier. Maybe Mallory was rubbing her nose in the affair."

"I just don't see her being a killer."

"Her fingerprints are at the scene," Burt said. "We don't even have that much concrete evidence against Joe."

"But, she lived in the house. Her prints are all over the place." Tom shook his head. "Even the crime scene investigator said that."

"I'm only concerned with the prints on the weapon." Burt finished his drink. "Let's bring her in and ask."

"All right." Tom sighed and followed him out the door. "You're the sergeant."

Mrs. Santiago answered the door.

"Good morning, ma'am. Is Mrs. Barnes home?" Tom smiled.

"Yes." She opened the door and the two detectives waited in the entryway while the maid went to get Sarah.

"Yes, officers, how can I help you?"

"Sorry, to disturb you, Mrs. Barnes, but we have a few questions for you."

"I'm happy to help." She waved her arm indicating the living room. "Do you want to come in?"

"Thank you, but I'm afraid we need to take you down to the station and talk there."

"Am I under arrest?" She looked scared.

"No," Burt said. "But this is a formal questioning. It needs to be done at the station."

"Do I need a lawyer?"

"Not at this time. If at any time you feel you want one, you will be allowed to call." Tom tried to sound friendly.

"This way, Mrs. Barnes." Burt led her to the un-marked car.

After entering the police station, they took her to an interrogation room.

"Do you want something to drink?" Tom offered.

"No, thank you."

Burt flipped the recorder on. "Now, we need to know where you were the night your sister was killed."

"I already told you I was in my room."

"You were there all night?"

"Yes. I'd just buried my daughter and wanted to be alone." The golden specks in her hazel eyes sparkled with tears. "I took a sedative and went to sleep."

"No one checked on you?"

"If someone came in, I wouldn't have heard them."

"You see, the problem is that no one can account for your whereabouts."

"Is there a reason I need to account for my activities?"

"We found your fingerprints at the crime scene," Burt said. "On the broken glass."

"Your print was also found on the weapon," Tom Added.

Sarah sat silently for a few moments. "I live there and my prints are on most of the items in the house."

"Yes, but having them on the glass by the body and on the murder weapon is too much of a coincidence," Burt said. "You have the same motives as your husband."

"We just want to get the truth," Tom said.

"I... I didn't mean to do it," Sarah sobbed.

Tom and Burt looked at each other surprised.

"I went downstairs to get a drink and Mallory came in the back door. We got into a huge fight. She accused me of killing our mother and said I deserved everything I got. She gloated about sleeping with my husband and didn't care that she'd killed my baby." Sarah cried harder.

"She laughed at me and turned to walk away. I had the glass in my hand and without thinking I threw it at her. It smacked her head and shattered. She turned around and started calling me names. I felt so hurt and angry. How dare she take everything away from me! Then stand there acting like it's my fault. I don't really remember what happened next. But I must have grabbed the knife off the counter and stabbed her."

"What did you do with the clothes you were wearing?"

"I washed them and put them in my dresser."

"Washing them wouldn't get rid of the blood," Tom said.

"I wasn't thinking clearly." Sarah looked at them. "I don't recall getting much blood on my clothes anyway."

"Did you get blood on the pictures?" Burt crossed his arms on the table. "Is that why you took them?

"What pictures?"

"Were there any pieces of paper or cloth around Mallory when you stabbed her?" Tom asked.

"I don't think so, but the whole thing is a blur." Sarah dried her eyes. "I didn't mean to kill her, it just happened."

"I understand," Tom said. "You just snapped."

"Yes." Sarah looked relieved. "I just couldn't let her keep hurting people."

"I know." Burt patted her hand. "It's going to be all right."

"What am I going to do now?" Sarah wiped a tear away.

"We're going to take you down to processing. You'll be allowed to call your dad." Burt continued to hold her hand until a woman officer escorted her away.

"That was the easiest interrogation we've ever done," Tom crossed his arms.

"She is overwhelmed with guilt," Burt commented.

"Not something we run into every day."

"No wonder she posted bail for her husband, she knew he was innocent." Burt scratched his chin. "Something still doesn't feel right."

"Why? Because we got the killer so fast?" Tom angled his lean body back into the chair.

"You're mad because I win the bet." Burt teased. "Joe didn't kill Mallory."

"What if she's covering for Joe?" Tom looked through the file. "What if they did it together?"

"Why do you still think Joe's involved?"

"The missing pictures." Tom looked at Burt. "What happened to the pictures?"

"It's possible Sarah took them and just can't remember."

"I don't think she'd forget seeing those images," Tom said.

"Besides we're not positive that the pictures were around the body," Burt pointed out.

"We found one under the body." Tom rested his chin on his folded hands. "It's a good guess there were more."

"Then let's find out what happened to the missing pictures and wrap up this case." Burt stood and slapped Tom's back.

Chapter 14

Joe burst into the police station. "I need detectives McCallahand and Wallace."

"Well, Burt Wallace is a sergeant not a detective," the officer manning the front station informed him.

"I don't care if he's the head clown at the circus, I want to talk to him." Joe ran an agitated hand through his thick, blond hair.

"What's all the racket?" Tom McCallahand walked into the room.

"Sarah didn't kill Mallory." Joe rushed toward the detective. "I did."

"Okay, hold on." Tom scratched the back of his head. "Come with me."

Joe followed him to a large desk cluttered with folders, papers and pictures. Burt Wallace was typing on the computer.

"Mr. Barnes says he killed Mallory Dillingham," Tom said as he sat in his chair.

"What?" Burt furrowed his gray brows. "Your wife already confessed to the crime."

"She's lying to protect me."

Tom's brows rose slightly and a small smirk formed at the corner of his mouth.

"Why would she do that?" Burt asked.

"I don't know." Joe paced around the small space. "I just know she didn't do it."

"But you said you didn't kill her earlier," Tom pointed out.

"I lied!"

"So we're supposed to believe you now?"

"Take my statement. I'm telling you I killed Mallory. She broke up my marriage and killed my baby. I wanted to get her back." Joe's brown eyes darkened, pleading with them.

"As convincing as you sound, I'm not buying it," Burt stated.

"But it's the truth." Joe took a couple deep breaths. "You can't lock up an innocent woman."

"But you want us to lock up an innocent man?" Tom said.

"I'm not innocent. Look at my life. I know you've seen the records from my past. Why would you think someone as sweet and loving as Sarah could kill her sister, and not believe someone with a history like mine would be a better suspect?"

"If you were truly guilty, you'd be trying to cover it up, not trying to convince us you did it." Burt pointed out.

"What if I give you proof." Joe looked them in the eye.

"Like what?"

Joe pulled out some crumbled photos and tossed them on the desk. "The missing pictures you're looking for."

"Why do we have two people in custody for this murder?" The DA, John Campbell, asked.

"They both confessed," Tom explained.

"What does the evidence say?"

"They both have a motive, but Sarah's finger-prints are at the crime scene," Burt said.

"And Joe gave us the missing pictures." Tom handed the DA the photos.

"Did you happen to notice the absence of blood?" John pointed out.

"Yes." Burt sighed.

"These pictures could have come from anywhere. There's nothing tying them to the murder scene. And the fingerprints will be hard to pinpoint."

"How did Joe know we were looking for the pictures?" Tom asked.

Burt looked at John. "We never said anything to him."

"Maybe Sarah said something to him," John suggested.

"She only had one phone call. Do you think she called him instead of her father?"

"I don't care who she called or how Joe knew about the pictures," John sighed. "I want an arrest that will stick."

"What are we supposed to do?" Burt asked. "They both confessed and neither one wants to recant."

"I think they're protecting each other," John said. "We need to cut one loose." He looked at both detectives. "Keep digging. There has to be solid evidence somewhere that reveals who really killed her. As it stands this is all circumstantial and I don't have a case."

"The confession should be enough to put someone away," Tom said.

"Which one?" The prosecutor tossed the bag of pictures onto the desk. "This case is turning into a three ring circus."

"All we need now is a fat lady to sing." Burt laughed.

"This isn't funny. The media are having a field day with this case and the Galveston PD are going to look like idiots if we don't solve this quickly."

"I'm more concerned about putting the right person behind bars than what the media think or say," Tom said.

"Then find evidence to shed some light on the real killer."

"We're still working on a few leads from the weapon," Burt said.

"Good. Keep me informed."

Robert walked into his dad's office and sat down on the leather couch, waiting for Richard to get off the phone. When the conversation ended, Richard slammed the phone down.

"Your sister has confessed to killing Mallory."

"I heard." Robert looked tired, haggard.

"Then Joe confessed." Richard threw his hands up in the air. "And they still haven't released Sarah."

"Are they trying to figure out who really killed Mallory?"

"You know Joe did it." Richard slammed his fists on the desk. "Why wouldn't they believe Sarah over that worthless piece of garbage?"

"You really believe Joe did it?"

"Yes. He was lurking around and I confronted him around six. He has no alibi after that. Then he's found sneaking out the door at eleven."

"But that's my point. Mallory had been dead for hours by the time he went into the kitchen."

"So he could have killed her earlier then came back."

"So he could trip over the body in the dark and make noise that would wake up the household?" Robert shook his head. "If he killed Mallory, I think he would have stayed away and not drawn attention to himself."

"Do you think Sarah did it?" Richard yelled.

"I don't know." Robert stood, pacing in a small circle. "But lots of people had reason to kill her including us." He stopped pacing and stared at his father.

"You think I killed her?" Richard arched a bushy brow.

"She did steal the company away from you by force. Money is always a powerful motive."

"You should know me better than that." Richard sounded hurt. "I've never put money above family." His hazel-brown eyes bore into his son. "Plus, I would have won the company back in court."

"I know you'd never put money above us kids but strangers won't know that."

"What motive did you have?" Richard looked confused.

"Mallory blackmailed me into siding with her."

Richard said nothing for a long time. "What could she possibly have on you?"

"She had photos of me in a compromising position with a young lady. She threatened to send them to the tabloids and ruin my chance of becoming state representative."

Richard shook his head. "I never knew Mallory had such an interest in photography."

"Only if it served her purpose." Robert sat down. "I know how Joe feels. The only difference is someone killed Mallory before she could destroy me as she did him."

"I'm not saying Mallory wasn't at fault, but that doesn't mean Joe didn't kill her." Richard sat down in his chair. "She made a lot of enemies. She was mean, ruthless and too ambitious for her own good." Richard exhaled loudly. "But I will never allow Sarah to go to prison."

"Even at the expense of an innocent man?" Robert let the question soak in. "I can't live with that, Dad."

"So, you're just going to throw your sister to the wolves?" Richard's voice demanded. "Don't you think she's been through enough already?"

"You sound like you believe she did it."

Richard opened his mouth to speak then stopped. "I don't know," he said softly.

"Like it or not, Joe is part of our family too." Robert got up to leave. "Sarah still loves him."

Richard sat in the silence of his office. Robert's words spinning like a drill bit, the truth hammering at his heart like the metal pipes that push through the rocky ground.

Joe sat on the cot in his cell, the walls closing in around him. He stood, but didn't have much room to pace. He felt cramped, a feeling that often overcame him since childhood. Probably due to the many times his mother had locked him into the tiny crawl space in the basement.

The fear of enclosed spaces was the main reason he'd loved working on the oil rigs. Although the work was hard, the open space and fresh air made up for the aches and pains of his body. Mallory's offer to move into an office had had no appeal to him at all. Besides the fact that he wasn't a paper pusher, he would have missed the outdoors.

He sighed and sat back down on his cot. Of course, now he'd be locked up for twenty years or more. *How has my life gotten so messed up*? He wondered. After working hard for years to overcome his childhood and make his life into something to be proud of, he'd ended up destroying everything good.

He now found himself in the lowest pits of hell, fighting his demons alone. Could he survive being locked up? Would he go insane?

"I'm already insane," he said to himself. How else could he explain his life right now?

The buzzing of the door opening interrupted his thoughts.

"You have a visitor," the guard said.

Joe felt his heart stop for a few seconds when he saw Sarah sitting on the other side of the glass. He pulled out the chair, sat down and picked up the phone. "Hey."

"Hey." Sarah smiled slightly. "How are you doing?"

"Fine. How are you?"

"Confused." She stared through the glass into his brown eyes. "Why did you confess?"

"Because I killed Mallory."

"No, you didn't." She tried to hold back the tears.

"I did."

"Stop saying that," Joe whispered. "You'd never have enough cruelty to kill anyone."

"I hated her." Sarah's soft tone turned harsh. "She took everything away from me and then laughed in my face." Tears rolled down her cheeks. "I felt so much hatred that I picked up the knife and stabbed her."

"It's not your fault, Sarah." Tears shimmered in his eyes. "This is all my fault. If I hadn't gotten drunk on New Year's Eve and slept with her, none of this would have happened."

"Mallory confessed that she loved you. She wanted to seduce you away from me."

"I allowed it to happen."

"Do you have any idea what your life is going to be like?" she asked.

"Yes."

"You're going to be locked up for years."

"I'm willing to suffer the consequence."

"I can't let you do that." Sarah looked away for a few seconds then looked into his eyes. "As much as it hurts thinking about you being with another woman, it hurts even more knowing you'd be locked up for a murder you didn't do."

"Shh." Joe put his finger to his lips. "They could be listening."

"I don't care. I've already told them I did it and they still let me go. Why won't anyone listen to me?"

"Think about it, Sarah." Joe pointed to his chest. "I'm a more believable suspect than you."

"Why? Because you're a man? Because you're stronger than me?" She shook her head. "I don't get it. I plunged that knife into her chest." She pointed to her chest. "I did it."

"I already have a record," Joe said. "I had the affair and I already admitted to forgery. It's not a long leap to conclude that I would do *anything* to keep you."

"Is that why you're doing this?" She leaned forward. "You're trying to protect me?"

"I couldn't protect you from the truth. I couldn't protect our daughter either." A tear slipped out of the corner of his eye. "Let me do something now."

"So, you're going to punish yourself by rotting away in a cramped cell? You think confessing to murder is going to absolve you of your guilt?"

"Nothing can absolve me of my guilt." He wiped a tear away and tried to smile, but couldn't.

"God can," Sarah stated.

"I don't want His forgiveness, I only want yours."

Sarah started crying. "I do forgive you, Joe."

Relief flooded over him faster than oil gushes from pipes. "That's more than I ever hoped for." He put his hand against the glass. "I love you."

"I love you too." Sarah placed her tiny hand against the glass too. "And that's why I can't let you do this. I know it will destroy you."

"Nothing can hurt me more than I'm already hurting."

"Being locked up is a death sentence for you."

"I can handle it."

"I won't let you." She shook her head. "I've always had other people protecting me. My whole life Dad, Robert, friends, you, even Mrs. Santiago has been there for me to lean on. They raised me, cleaned up after me, helped me and watched out for me. But, this time I have to stand on my own two feet. I have to take responsibility. I can't let you go to prison for my crime."

"Sarah, please just think about it," Joe begged.

"No. I have to do this." She rubbed her index finger up and down the glass, tracing his finger.

"I took a vow to love, honor, cherish and protect you." His heart ached. "I failed you in the first three, but I will protect you no matter what."

"You're human, Joe. You made a mistake." She locked eyes with him, love and forgiveness reaching through the glass, grasping his heart. "So did I." She started crying. "I snapped, Joe. I lost control and I took another human's life. It's my fault Mallory is dead and I can't allow you to destroy your life just to protect me when I'm guilty."

"You said that God would forgive me." Joe stared at her. "He'll forgive you too."

"I committed murder," Sarah insisted.

"I committed adultery," Joe countered. "They're both the same in God's eyes."

"I need to be a grown up," Sarah said. "I can't let you do this." She hung up the phone.

"Sarah, wait!" Joe yelled.

She walked away.

"I love you." He pounded on the plexiglass.

She turned and read his lips. "I love you too," she mouthed the words.

"Come on, Joe, we need every single detail from you." Tom sat down across from him.

"I've already told you what happened."

"Tell us again," Burt said. "There seem to be missing pieces of the puzzle and we need you to fill them in."

"We buried the baby. I went back to the hotel for a while then I decided to go see Sarah. I snuck ..."

"What time was that?" Burt asked.

"I'm not sure, around six or seven. I only remember the sun was going down."

"Anything else you remember?" Tom asked.

"I knew I wouldn't be welcome so I tried sneaking through the yard to avoid the camera that surveils the driveway. I hid in some bushes when the SUV came by."

"What SUV?" Burt sat up. "You never mentioned it before."

"I forgot. It's not a big deal. I recognized it as Mrs. Santiago's."

"So, what happened next?" Tom asked.

"I made it into the entry way then Richard stopped me."

"The two of you had words?"

"Yes. He wouldn't let me see Sarah."

"Then you left?"

"No." Joe looked the detective in the eye. "I went around back and came in through the kitchen door. Mallory was in the kitchen and we had a fight. I threw a glass at her then stabbed her."

"Why aren't your fingerprints on the murder weapon?"

"I wore gloves," Joe said. "Why are you trying to prove I didn't do it?"

"We're just filling in the missing questions," Tom said. "I believe you did it. I've thought you were the killer since we arrested you that night, but the prosecutor needs more evidence."

"What kind of gloves would you have in eighty degree weather?" Burt asked.

"Leather gloves. I use them at work."

"And you just happen to have them on when you committed this crime."

"They are always in my truck."

"Why did you have them on that night?"

Joe paused for a minute. "After I got caught, I knew the security guards would be watching. So, I went back to my truck and grabbed the gloves. I had intended to use them to cover the lens of the camera."

"So, how did they get into the kitchen?" Burt asked.

"I never noticed a camera on the way to the back door. So, they were in my pocket during the fight with Mallory."

"How many times did you stab her?"

"Three." Joe looked at Sargent Burt Wallace. "I stabbed her three times." Confidence rang in his voice.

"What did you do after you killed her?" Burt sat back in his chair, doubt showing in his posture.

"I got out of there. I knew I needed to set up some kind of alibi so I drove to the lake."

"Why did you come back?" Tom asked.

"When I never got a call, I wondered if anyone had found the body yet. So I went back and when I noticed that Mrs. Santigo's SUV was still gone, I figured she hadn't found the body yet."

"Mrs. Santiago is the one who caught you leaving." Burt furrowed his gray brow.

"I know. That surprised me too. That's why I was getting out of there," Joe explained.

"So you came back just to check on the body?" Tom asked.

"I wanted to make sure she was dead." Joe shrugged. "That woman was the devil I wouldn't have been surprised if she'd lived."

"Why don't the pictures have any blood on them?" Burt asked.

"She waved the pictures around in my face, gloating over how she'd destroyed my marriage. She said she was glad the baby had died and that now I had no ties to Sarah at all." His eyes burned a little. "It was the last straw. She turned to walk away and I grabbed the glass off the counter and threw it at her. She fell on the floor and the pictures scattered around her. Without even thinking I grabbed a knife and stabbed her. I noticed the pictures and picked them up. I couldn't throw them in the garbage because you would have found them. So, I wiped the blood off and got a plastic bag from the drawer."

"Why did you keep them?" Burt asked. "If I'd just killed someone and took evidence from the scene, I would have thrown them in the lake."

"I wasn't thinking," Joe confessed. "The whole thing happened so quickly. I never planned on killing anyone. She just made me so mad!"

"Why are you coming forward now, after denying it before?"

"I can't let Sarah take the blame for something I did."

"Funny, she's saying the same about you." Burt shook his head. "I think the two of you are trying to confuse us so we won't find out who really killed your sister-in-law."

"I don't care what you think, or what Sarah says. I killed Mallory and I've signed a statement. I believe after this meeting all the gaps are filled in. The case is closed." Joe stood. "I'm done answering your questions, I want to go back to my cell."

Another officer led Joe away.

"Are you buying any of that?" Burt asked.

"Most of it." Tom looked at Burt. "He knew how many stab wounds there were."

"He could have guessed." Burt shrugged. "Of course, he knew about the missing pictures before we said anything."

"Sarah didn't know anything about the pictures." Tom pointed out. "Should we see if she knows how many times her sister was stabbed?"

"I'm thinking we should take a look at the surveillance cameras. Let's see if we can find Joe sneaking around," Burt said.

"You're still looking for evidence to clear him. Why?" Tom looked confused.

"I don't know," Burt said. "My gut is telling me something isn't right."

"Maybe it's telling you it's hungry." Tom patted his stomach. "That's what mine is screaming."

"Your stomach is always screaming it's hungry." Burt stood. "I don't know how you stay so skinny?"

"I have big feet." Tom held up a size fifteen shoe. "All the food goes down there."

"Let's go big foot." Burt opened the door. "Maybe you'll quit being so cranky after you eat and see the evidence in a different light."

"I'm not cranky," Tom defended. "I just see the completed puzzle. You're not the only one who thinks something is missing."

Chapter 15

The two detectives watched more videos that had been found in Mallory's apartment. "I think she should have gone into the porn business," Tom said.

"She spends more time having sex than a prostitute," another officer said.

"Look at the dates," someone pointed out. "These tapes go back a couple of years."

"And some of them are about other people," Tom noticed.

"The only person she didn't film was her dad," someone said.

"And the maids," another cop said.

"No, just wait." Someone laughed. "There is a maid coming up."

No sooner had he said that and a camera flipped on, showing a young woman in a black and white maid's uniform. Her long curly hair was pulled back in a ponytail.

"Hey, didn't we interview her?" Tom asked. "That's Maria Santiago."

"How come you remember her name and didn't label her 'that maid', like you usually do?" Burt asked.

"She's hot." Tom took a bite of his sandwich. "I always remember hot girls' names."

"Oh, here we go." Someone yelled as a young man entered the closet.

The officers watched as the two lovers embraced and kissed. The passion exploded and clothes started to come off. The man pulled the tie from her hair, running his fingers through the long tresses. He turned and braced her against wall, giving the audience a full glimpse of his face.

"Wait a minute." Burt sat forward. "Stop it."

"No." someone else shouted. "This is the best part."

"I know that face." Burt went to the machine and pressed the rewind button then stopped it on the guys face. "That's Robert Dillingham."

Tom sat forward. "You're right."

"Hey, press the play button."

"Yeah, we want to finish watching the show."

"We have work to do," Burt tossed the rest of his sandwich into the garbage. "Let's go, Tom."

"I wanted to finish watching the evidence," Tom grumbled. He stuffed the rest of his food into his mouth. His cheeks puffed out like a squirrel's.

The two detectives walked into a chaos of political activity. The receptionist showed them into Robert's office.

"Mr. Dillingham." Burt shook his hand. "We have a few questions."

"Of course, come in." He waved a hand at the two chairs in front of his desk. "Have a seat." He sat behind his desk. "What can I do for you?"

"We've come across some evidence in your sister's murder case."

"Oh." Robert leaned back in his chair. "Something that clears Sarah of the charges?"

"Not exactly," Burt said. "But it does shed light on another suspect."

"Really?"

"I'm afraid so." Burt waited. He'd had years of experience watching the guilty. Suspects pretending that they had no idea of the evidence that had been uncovered.

After a few long seconds, Robert asked. "Are you going to fill me in, or sit here all day?"

"We need your alibi again," Tom said.

"I told you I was here."

"Can anyone verify that?"

"I'm afraid not." Robert sat forward. "Why?"

"It's just that while searching Mallory's apartment some videos turned up, and, well, you happen to be on one," Burt explained.

"What videos!" Robert jumped up.

"You and a certain hot maid, having sex in the closet," Tom said.

"Damn it!" Robert ran his hand through his short, brown hair and walked over to the window. "I thought she only had pictures of us."

"You knew about the pictures?" Burt asked.

Robert exhaled. "Mallory threatened to expose my affair with Maria if I didn't side with her on the take-over." Robert spun around. "It would have ruined my chance of becoming state representative."

"So, you sided with her?"

"Yes, that's how she got control of the company.

"Does your father know about this?" Tom asked.

"I told him about the blackmail the other night, but he doesn't know I love Maria." Robert looked deep in thought. "You said it was filmed in a closet?"

"Yes."

"She was one sick woman," Robert sighed.

"We need to ask you, one more time, where were you on the night she was killed." Burt flipped his note-book open.

"I was out with Maria then I came back here to get some work done."

"So, you're the friend she was trying to protect?" He jotted down a few notes.

"Yes."

"Did you see Mallory at all that night?"

"No. I hadn't seen her since the night Sarah went into the hospital."

"Do you know the whereabouts of the maid after your date?" Burt asked.

"Her name is Maria," Robert sounded upset. "I dropped her off at home and came back here."

"What time was that?" Burt flipped a few pages, checking his previous notes.

"I don't know. I didn't punch a time clock." Robert ran a hand through his hair, again. "I got here around seven."

"So she was home by six-thirty or so?"

"I guess." Robert looked at his watch. "Why does it matter? Joe already confessed."

"So did your sister." Tom pointed out.

"Sarah didn't kill anyone and neither did I."

"That remains to be seen."

"Joe needs your help." Sarah crossed her arms and sat back against the couch.

"Why should I help him?" Richard's square jaw clamped tight.

"He didn't kill Mallory."

"So you say, but the police have evidence."

"They have evidence against me, too."

"None of this would have happened if he'd kept his pants zipped up."

"Like he had a chance with Mallory chasing after him?" She fought back the emotions rolling inside and focused on the task at hand. "You know as well as I do that marriage vows never meant anything to Mallory. She'd been after Joe since the day we married."

"He could have resisted."

"He was drunk, Dad." She stood, softening her voice and her pose. Walking over to Richard, she laid a hand on his shoulder. "He made a mistake, are you going to punish him forever?"

"I don't understand how you can just forgive him like nothing happened."

"Because I love him."

Richard shook his head. "You've always been too forgiving." He placed his hand over hers and squeezed.

"I have reasons to forgive him." She squeezed back. "I know he still loves me."

"And you want me to pay for a lawyer to get him off?"

"He needs the best."

"I don't think he's worth it."

"Will you trust my judgment?"

"I'm sorry, Princess, but I never liked the idea of you marrying him in the first place."

"Why, because he's poor?" She withdrew her hand and paced a few steps away.

"Money had nothing to do with it. But, he's a roughneck and not just as a job description. He's loud, rowdy and likes chasing women."

"He's also gentle, honest and hardworking. Except for Mallory, he's been faithful to me and I owe it to him to get the best counsel we can afford."

"Are you going to divorce him?"

"No."

"What if he goes to prison?"

"I'll wait for him."

"You are the most stubborn female." Richard threw his arms up in the air. "I don't know what to do with you."

"I have proof he didn't kill her." She turned to face her father. "I know for a fact he's innocent."

"I don't want to hear it." Richard turned to look out the window. He didn't like the look in his daughter's eyes.

"Dad, you need to know that I ..."

"No!" Richard yelled. "I don't want to hear it."

"But I ..."

He spun around sharply. "Don't say another word. I will not allow you to take the blame for this dreadful crime."

"But I ..." She tried one more time.

"Enough!"

"You can't shut out the truth," Sarah said quietly.

"You can't invent a story just to get your cheating husband off."

"He's willing to go to prison for me." She let the truth sink in. "You know his fear of enclosed spaces. Prison will be the worst torture for him. He'd be better off with a death sentence."

"That suits me just fine."

"You're impossible." Sarah stormed to the door then turned and said, "If you could just put your anger aside, you'd see the truth."

Richard's gaze met her hers. "You really love him that much?"

"I do." She didn't hesitate.

"You're willing to waste your life waiting for a criminal to get out of prison."

"That's the point, Dad. He's not a criminal."

"But, you'd wait for him?"

"Yes." She left.

Richard turned back to the window. Why had his kids turned out so hard-headed?

The criminal investigator sprayed a liquid on the pictures then turned on a blue light. "There's no blood on these pictures at all," she said. "Even if the blood had been wiped off, the Luminol would show the blood splatter."

"These pictures aren't from the crime scene," Burt said. "I knew it!"

"That doesn't prove he's innocent," Tom argued.

"Why would he lie?" Burt asked.

"Exactly, why would he confess to murder and hand us proof if he didn't do it?"

"How many criminals do you know, who just walk in, confess and hand us proof?"

"Not many," Tom said. "But it didn't take much for Sarah to confess, either. We told her that her fingerprints were at the crime scene and she spilled her guts."

"And after that Joe barges in, confessing," Burt said. "He's trying to protect his wife."

"Or, she's trying to protect him," Tom said. "Either way, we have this case wrapped up. One of them did it."

"The prosecutor needs more evidence." Burt reminded him. "He wants to have definite proof against one of them."

"So, that's why we're still wasting time with this case?"

"That and I want to see the right person go to jail," Burt said.

"It's not our job to save some poor schmuck from himself."

"It's our job to reveal the truth

The criminal investigator returned from the back room, holding a folder. "I've finished running the test on the cleaners from the Dillingham house." She handed Tom the folder. "None of them use petroleum. They are all plant based cleaners, a line of green products."

"So?" Tom asked.

"How did the petroleum get on the handle?" Burt asked.

"Joe said he wore work gloves." Tom pointed out.

"That could explain the dirt too," she agreed. "However there was something else that seemed very interesting." She folded her arms. "The cleaners for the floors and sinks all had palm oil and lactic acid. The only cleaner that had the xanthan gum was the toilet bowl cleaner. The gum makes it thick so it sticks against the bowl."

"So, the knife was in the bathroom?" Tom asked.

"Somehow toilet bowl cleaner got onto the knife," the investigator said.

"I don't see what that has to do with the case?" Tom looked at his partner. "But, I guess we'll be checking it out."

"Very true."

Joe hesitated when he saw his father-in-law sitting at the window. He wished the guards would have told him who his visitor was before dragging him down here. He didn't want to be rude, so he sat down and mentally prepared himself as he picked up the phone.

"Richard," Joe said.

"How are you doing?"

Joe raised a blond brow in surprise. "Umm, fine."

"I had a talk with Sarah."

So that was the reason for the visit.

"She wants me to hire the best defense attorney to get you off."

"But I've confessed," Joe said. "There won't be a trial."

"She says she won't recant her confession unless we can get you off."

"Listen, Richard." Joe sat forward. "You've got to talk to her. Tell her to stop with this confession thing."

"I've tried, but she's stubborn and won't listen." Richard sighed. "She thinks you're innocent."

"It doesn't matter what she thinks or says," Joe said. "I will go to prison and there's nothing she can do to stop it."

"Did you kill Mallory?" Richard stared at Joe.

Joe looked deep inside the man sitting across from. He'd always respected his honesty and integrity. "It was my fault." The answer was honest. He knew Richard would see through anything false.

"It wasn't all your fault." Richard sat in silence for a long time. "I'm as much to blame for your daughter's death as anybody else."

"You?" Joe's thick brows knit together.

"I didn't make Mallory move out because I was mad about the takeover. I admit I was furious, and frustrated with her, but I was worried about Sarah and the baby. I had a gut feeling that something had been going on between the two of you. Mallory's behavior toward Sarah had been getting worse. When the doctor told us she needed to have less stress in her life, I knew Mallory would push every button so I asked her to move out."

"But you did that to protect Sarah," Joe said. "What does that have to do with the baby?"

"When Mallory showed up for dinner, I should have made her leave. I knew she was up to something and I let it go." Richard's voice cracked. "I should have never allowed her to visit Sarah. If I'd only made her leave, my granddaughter would still be alive and Mallory too."

"No one knew what Mallory had in mind."

"I was her father, I should have known."

"Did you ever think she'd be capable of stealing the company away from you the way she did?" Joe asked.

"No."

"Did you ever think that she'd seduce men just to blackmail them into doing her bidding?"

"No."

"Then how can you possibly think you would have known what scheme she planned that night?"

"I should have known all of that about her. She was my child after all."

"Mallory only let people see the side of her she wanted. She was a master manipulator. No one knew the true darkness that lurked deep inside her."

"I just don't understand why? Why was she so full of hatred and evil?"

"No one can answer that, not even Mallory. I believe some people are born good and some are born bad, so... is there really a choice in the matter?" Joe asked.

"I do believe that. People choose their own path," Richard said. "Every decision we make molds us into the people we are supposed to be."

"Well, then, Mallory choose the wrong path." Joe looked into Richard's eyes. "There was nothing you could have done."

"But there's something I can do now. I can get you out of here."

"You can try, but I don't think it'll work," Joe sighed. "I think you're better off saving your money and forgetting about me."

"Sarah says she's going to wait for you, even if you go to prison."

"She'll get tired of waiting and give up." His heart hurt at that thought. Even though he wanted her to go on with her life, a part of him wanted her to remember him, to be waiting when and if he ever got released.

"You don't know how strong willed she is." Richard laughed. "She got that from her mother."

"Right." Joe smiled.

"I just have one more question?" Richard looked right into Joe's heart. "Do you love my daughter?"

"From the moment I laid eyes on her."

"Then, I'll see what I can do about getting you out of here."

"Thank you, sir." But Joe held little hope that anything could be done.

The DA stormed into the detective's office. "What the hell is this?" He held a paper in his hand, his chubby cheeks stained red.

"I guess, now, it truly is a three ring circus," Tom said. "Earlier it was only a two ring circus."

"This isn't funny." John paced a few steps forward, slamming the papers down on the desk. "How many more people are going to confess to this murder?"

"Is there anyone else left?" Tom quirked a brow.

The DA glared. "Why is Richard Dillingham confessing to this crime?" He sat down.

"Maybe he's trying to get his daughter off the hook?" Burt suggested.

"Her husband has already confessed," John reminded them. "I think they're trying to mess this case up."

"I would think the father of the victim would want justice," Tom said.

"Richard did have a motive. His own flesh and blood stole the family company right out from under him," Burt pointed out.

"He also says that he blamed Mallory for Sarah going to the hospital and the baby dying." John read the confession. "Grief can be a powerful motive to kill."

"Are you buying his confession?" Tom asked.

"I don't know." He skimmed over the paper. "He does admit to wiping the handle off with his handkerchief."

"We have it at the lab right now," Burt said. "That would be consistent with earlier reports that the handle has been wiped clean."

"Plus, red threads had been stuck on the handle and his handkerchief was red," Tom noted.

"Why would he keep it?" The DA asked.

"The most damaging piece of evidence is the pictures." Burt handed the DA photos of the bloodied pictures. "They are being examined too."

"You think these are the real pictures from the crime scene?"

"They do have blood on them," Burt said. "The lab is trying to match up the splatter pattern."

"But the splatter isn't clear now since the blood has been smudged," Tom added.

"So, you think he really killed his daughter?" John asked.

"I do believe him when he says that he needed to protect one child from the other." Burt shrugged. "It's got to be hard for a father to see your child turn out to be so evil."

"This is the most confusing case I've ever worked on," John complained. "They all three have good reasons to kill her, and all three have confessed." He tossed the photos down. "Have any of them recanted their confession?

"No. Do you want us to keep digging?" Tom asked.

"Yes."

"We still have a few other leads to follow, maybe they'll lead to the real killer," Burt said.

"I hope so," the DA sighed. "This case is giving me indigestion."

Chapter 16

"Dad, what are you doing?" Sarah said into the phone. "You didn't kill Mallory."

"I'm protecting you," Richard said. "The way I should have the night Mallory told you about the affair."

"That wasn't your fault."

"They have enough evidence to use against me." Richard assured her. "I found Mallory right before Joe came in. I saw the pictures scattered around her body and thought they could be used against you, so I picked them up and used my handkerchief to wipe off the handle." He looked at Sarah through the plexiglass. "Apparently I didn't do a very good job."

"So they can get you for tampering with evidence, but that doesn't prove you killed her."

"I thought it was a stroke of luck when I heard Joe coming in the back door," Richard continued. "I shut the lights off and waited in the hallway. I was waiting for the right time to walk in and surprise him, but Mrs. Santiago beat me to it. My plan was a perfect: if they convicted him, you'd be free."

"You knew I did it?" Her eyes widened. "How?"

"I saw you run by the office door earlier that evening. You were sobbing uncontrollably. At first, I thought you knew Joe had come by and that was why you were so upset. I started to go after you to make sure you were all right, but decided to leave you alone. You'd already had such a hard day and I wanted you to rest. Later, I went to the kitchen for a snack and found Mallory."

"Why blame Joe?"

"He seemed as good a scape goat as anyone. Plus, I blamed him for all the hurt he caused you."

"It sounds like you had the perfect plan, so why are you detouring from it now?"

"Because you confessed and won't stop until they lock you up."

"But, I did it, Dad. I deserve to be punished." Tears filled her eyes.

"No one can blame you for your rage, not after what Mallory put you through."

"You can't protect me," Sarah insisted.

"I'm not. Joe beat me to it, now I'm trying to right the wrong I did against him."

"Joe isn't going to allow this any more than I am."

"You said that he won't last being locked up. At first I didn't care and thought he deserved it, but now I know that's not fair. If you love him, then you two need to be together."

"That's not fair to you," Sarah said. "None of this is fair."

"Listen to me baby girl." Richard tapped the plexiglass to get her eyes on him. "You need to tell the detectives that you only confessed to save Joe. They'll believe you. With my statement they will let him go and there will only be one confession. Mine."

"I can't do that, Dad." She shook her head.

"You and Joe have been punished enough. It's time the two of you start living your life."

"I'm not letting you give up your life to save us." Tears flowed down her cheeks.

"I'm an old man. It makes more sense for me to take the wrap than you or Joe." He looked into her eyes. "Besides, I'm going to have the best lawyers money can buy."

"No. This isn't right."

"Sarah, I'm your father and you need to do as I say. I'm telling you I killed Mallory." His tone was stern.

"You're going to recant your confession and forget all this guilt. You don't deserve to suffer any more."

Sarah wiped her tears away. "Why is it that I'm always bringing you pain?"

"What in blazes are you talking about?" Richard's forehead creased.

"Ever since I was born, I've brought you nothing but pain. I killed my mother. I've fought you nonstop about the oil business ruining the environment. Mallory and I were always fighting and now you're in jail because of me."

"Princess, you have been the light in my life. You were a light to your mother also, that's why she chose to give birth to you. I wouldn't trade one minute of my life with you.

"As for your fight for the environment, I couldn't be more proud of you. I raised you to stand up for your beliefs and you've worked hard at doing that. I admire your strength, determination and commitment to your family and the environment." Richard wiped his forehead

"I love you, Dad."

"I love you, too." He looked at his baby girl, all grown up. "Let me do this."

"I can't," she sighed. "It wouldn't be right."

"Stubborn." He smiled. "Just like your mother."

"What are the police doing here again?" Maria asked. She walked over to the counter, setting the blue grocery bags down.

"They are looking through the house and checking the vehicles." Mrs. Santiago dabbed at her eyes with a tissue.

"Mom, what's wrong?" Maria walked over and put her arm around her mother's shoulders.

"It's Mr. Dillingham," she said. "He's confessed to the murder."

"What?" Maria's arm dropped. "I thought Joe confessed."

"Yes, he did, so did Sarah."

"Why are the police snooping around if they have three confessions?"

"I don't know. I think they are trying to find more evidence or something." Mrs. Santiago blew her nose in the tissue.

"I don't think it's legal for them to be here." Maria crossed her arms. "Do they have a search warrant?"

"Apparently they don't need one." Mrs. Santiago started helping put the groceries away. "Sarah gave them permission."

"Can she do that?" Maria asked. "I mean, it's Mr. Dillingham's house."

"She lives here so I guess it's okay. Besides she's hoping they will find evidence to prove Mr. Dillingham is innocent."

"You don't believe Mr. Dillingham did it, do you?"

"No."

"Why would he say he did it?" Maria went back to putting the groceries away.

"To protect Sarah."

"Why are the police searching the cars?" Maria sounded agitated.

"I don't know," Mrs. Santiago said. "They asked me if they could look through mine."

"What! How could you allow them to search through your personal things?"

"Because I want to help prove no one in this house killed Mallory. I have nothing to hide."

"What's the big deal, anyway?" Maria slammed a cupboard door. "The world is better off with Mallory Dillingham dead."

"Maria!" Mrs. Santiago's dark eyes widened.

"What? It's the truth." She crossed her arms. "I'm tired of my life being disrupted."

"That is the most selfish remark I've ever heard," she scolded. "Someone is dead."

"A mean, selfish, back stabbing, evil someone." Maria slammed another door. "I don't see why the police even care. Why can't they just forget about her and move on. I'm sure there are more important cases to work on."

"You are sounding just like Mallory." Mrs. Santiago shook her head. "Not one compassionate bone in your body."

"How dare you compare me with that witch."

"Then listen to yourself." She stared at her daughter. "I don't care what Mallory said or did, no one deserves to be killed like that." Mrs. Santiago put her hand on her stomach. "No one should be stabbed so violently."

"Mom, are you alright?" Maria came to her side.

Mrs. Santiago bent over slightly. "It's too much to take in."

"Sit down." Maria steered her to a chair.

"I can't believe she's gone." Mrs. Santiago started crying. "I remember when they brought her home from the hospital. She was so small and so innocent."

"What happened to her after she grew up?" Maria mumbled.

"I don't know. But it's so tragic," Mrs. Santiago sighed. "A tragic ending to a tragic life."

Maria shook her head. "The only thing tragic about Mallory was the destruction she caused everyone else."

"She wasn't always that way. She used to be a bright, beautiful child, who loved flowers and dirt. I remember her starting a lemonade stand and charging five dollars a glass, when she was eight." Mrs. Santiago shook her head. "So ambitious, even back then."

"In the end her ambition caught up with her."

The police entered the kitchen.

"Mrs. Santiago, can you come down to the station for more questioning?" Burt Wallace asked.

"Why?" Maria looked worried. "My mother didn't do anything."

"We found new evidence and need to get some answers."

"It's all right, Maria." Mrs. Santiago stood.

"I'll call Robert," Maria said as her mother walked out the door.

"We need you to go over the entire day again," Tom McCallahand said.

"I've already told you this," Mrs. Santiago sighed.

"Can you explain how blood got in your SUV?"

"What?" Her dark eyes widened. "There's no blood in my car."

"Not now because you cleaned it up. But the Luminol found traces on the passenger seat and the steering wheel."

"I don't know." Her dark eyes filled with shock. "But I assure you I didn't kill Mallory. She was like a daughter to me."

"Would you kill her in order to protect your own daughter?" Tom leaned closer. "After all, blood is thicker than oil."

"What are you talking about?" She wiped her eyes. "Why would I kill Mallory? What would I be protecting Maria from?"

Burt opened a folder, withdrawing a picture and handed it to her. "Mallory was blackmailing Robert about his affair with Maria."

"Did you know about the two of them?" Tom asked.

Mrs. Santiago bowed her head. "Yes, but I didn't know anything about the blackmail." She looked up at Burt. "Is that why Robert voted with Mallory on the takeover?"

"Yes."

"But I didn't know anything about that," she insisted.

"How long have you known they were dating?"

"Only a few months. I caught them kissing and Maria finally told me the truth."

"Did Mr. Dillingham know about the affair?"

"I don't know." Her eyes turned cold. "Why don't you ask him?"

"Mrs. Santiago we are trying to find a killer." Burt stood and paced a few steps. "I need you to tell me about anything out of the ordinary that day."

"Are you kidding?" Her tone rose an octave. "We buried Sarah's baby girl, then had a wake at the house. I did some cleaning, ran a few errands and went to bed. I heard a loud noise in the kitchen and walked in to find

Mallory dead on the floor." Her dark eyes bore into the sergeant. "Is that enough out of the ordinary for you?"

"What kind of cleaning did you do?" Tom asked.

Mrs. Santiago rolled her eyes, as much to remember as for the tediousness of the interview. "I cleared the dining room and loaded the dishwasher. I vacuumed the living room then cleaned the two bathrooms downstairs. I went to the drug store and the dry cleaners. Then I came home and went to bed."

"Where did you park when you came home?" Burt asked.

"In the driveway." Her lips pinched tight as something stuck her memory.

"Do you remember something?" Burt asked.

"No." She shook her head. "I just remembered I didn't park in the driveway. I parked on the street."

"Why?" Tom asked.

"The street is closer to the service entrance.

"Didn't you have laundry to carry in?"

"Only a few shirts and a dress."

"So you'd rather carry the dry cleaning all the way around the house than park in the driveway?" Burt crossed his arms. "What about the blood?"

"I don't know." Her face flushed red.

"I think you're lying," Tom said.

"I think you're protecting someone," Burt said.

"I'm not!" Mrs. Santiago yelled. "I don't know who killed Mallory."

"Who are you protecting?"

"No one."

"Are you willing to go to prison?"

"I didn't do it." Her dark skin went pale. "I swear."

"Maybe so, but helping the real murderer makes you an accessory after the fact."

"I'm not hiding anything."

"Really?" Burt asked. "Then where are the gloves?"

Her dark brows knit together. "What gloves?"

"The rubber gloves you wore while cleaning."

"I don't know. I put them in the sink to dry and they were gone the next morning." Confusion danced in her eyes. "Why are you worried about rubber gloves?"

"Did you throw them away?" Tom asked.

"No, but one of the other maids may have."

"Did Maria throw them away?"

"No." She said confidently. "Maria wouldn't touch those gloves, she's allergic to ..." She stopped in mid-sentence. "Well, she might have picked them up to throw them in the trash can."

"Changing your story again?"

"I'm just trying to answer all these questions. You're confusing me."

"People only get confused when they are trying to keep their lies straight."

"I'm not saying anything else." She crossed her arms under her chest, lifting sad, defiant eyes to Sergeant Burt Wallace. "Besides, you already have more than enough people confessing, why are you bothering me?"

"We want the right person to be punished."

"Well it's not me or Maria."

"We're going to let you go now, but don't leave town."

Mrs. Santiago stood, keeping her back straight, she left with as much dignity as she could muster.

"What do you think, Burt?" The DA took a bite of his sandwich.

"She's covering for someone."

"More than likely her daughter," Tom said.

"What makes you think that?" John swallowed the last bite of his lunch. "She could have just as easily done it."

"Naah, she's not that good an actor," Tom said. "She is obliviously lying."

"Yeah," Burt agreed. "She changed her story in the middle of the interview, almost like something clicked and the pieces fell into place."

"Too bad you couldn't get her to reveal that puzzle," John said.

"That would make your job too easy." Burt smiled. "Then you'd be slacking all day."

John wiped his mouth, crinkled the paper napkin and tossed it into the brown bag. "Right, I'm slacking so much I don't even have time for a decent lunch. And when I do start eating, you guys come and give me indigestion."

"I have some Rolaids," Tom offered.

"That won't help my ulcer, besides I'd rather have evidence of the real killer."

"We're working on it," Burt said. "There's also the matter of the rubber gloves."

"What gloves?" John perked up.

"Maria Santiago told us she's allergic to regular rubber gloves, but had to use them because they were out of her special gloves," Tom said.

"However, we found a closet full of her gloves," Burt added.

"So, she lied?" John shrugged his shoulders. "Maybe they bought them after the murder."

"We're looking into it. We just need a little more time," Tom said.

"I'm afraid if we take any longer the suspect list is going to be longer than Burt's nose."

"Hey!" Burt scrunched his nose up. "It's not that long."

"Yeah, right, that's like saying the Aspen ski slope is just a bunny trail." Tom laughed.

"I don't care what you have to do but bring me some hard evidence, a confession, anything that I can use in court. Get back to the interviews and get the evidence I need.

"Yes, sir." Burt and Tom both saluted.

Joe picked up his personal belongings and headed out the door. The thick, balmy night smothered his senses like a blanket of oil. He inhaled deeply, relishing the fresh air and his freedom. He could breath, not feeling smothered by bars and walls. No longer feeling wrapped in a cocoon of stifled air.

He felt his muscles unclench, letting go of the tension that had built up over the last few days. He rolled his head from side to side then stretched his arms over his head. All the fear and anxiety slowly departed into the June air.

Overhead the moon hung in the dark sky looking like a crystal ball wrapped in a blue velvet cloak, while the wide expanse of asphalt stretched before him in a cracked glory of faded gray. He'd never been so happy to see a parking lot.

As joyful as he felt at finally having his freedom, nothing compared to the sight of the long, black limousine pulling into the old parking lot. The driver honked wildly.

When the car slowed down, Sarah jumped out of the back, not even waiting for the car to fully stop.

"Joe," she called, waving her hands in the air as if he couldn't see her.

His heart nearly leapt out of his chest at the bright smile fastened to her face. Her oval face outshone the moon. "Sarah," he barely breathed her name. He stood transfixed to the spot, in awe of the fact that she'd come to pick him up.

"Joe!" She ran towards him.

"Sarah!" He sprinted to close the distance. He picked her up as if she were a doll and swung her around in a wide circle. "I'm not dreaming. It's really you."

"It's really me." She laid her hands on each side of his cheek. The rough stubble pricked her delicate skin.

"I didn't think I'd ever see you again." His eyes drank in her dainty features, devouring her creamy skin and honey colored hair.

"I told you I was coming."

"I'm so sorry, Sarah. I promise I'm never going to hurt you again. I'll spend the rest of my life making you happy. I've missed you so much."

"Me too." Her soft pink lips gently traced the corner of his mouth. "I've already forgiven you, Joe. I don't want anything except your love." She gently bit the bottom of his lip. "I'm not about to let Mallory ruin everything we've worked so hard for."

The hunger welled up in Joe. It'd been far too long since he'd tasted her sweetness. As much as he wanted to handle her gently, he couldn't control his passion. It arose within like a beast roaring for food. He deepened the kiss, his tongue searching out the pleasure he knew was stored there.

Sarah groaned with each kiss. His lips captured every sob, devouring her tenderness and pressing his lips even harder to hers. The kiss seemed to go on forever. Lips touching, tongues dancing and hands roaming, they continued their tango until their mouths felt numb.

Joe pulled his mouth away from hers and smiled. Then, his lips traced a line along her neck and collar bone. The creaminess of her skin sent shivers through his heart. "I love you," he said against her neck.

"Joe." Her voice was soft.

His heart stopped for a second or two. Had she come to her senses and realized she didn't want a louse like him? His lips pursed in a straight line, waiting for the browbeating he rightly deserved. His eyes searched her face for some sign.

"You might want to put me down. My legs are going numb."

"Sorry." Breathing a sigh of relief, he let her small body slide along his until her feet touched the ground. The movement coaxed a gasp from Sarah. She locked eyes with him and smiled slyly, realizing the effect she had on him.

"Are you ready to come home?" Laying a hand against his chest, she felt his muscles jerk to attention like a soldier.

Home, he never thought he'd hear that word falling from her lips. "Yes."

She took his hand and led him toward the limousine.

"I can't believe you brought this monstrosity of a car," Joe teased. "Where's your smart car?"

"At home." The chauffeur opened the door and Sarah slid into the car.

"Aren't you afraid that this gas guzzling machine is ruining the ozone layer?" Joe asked as he settled in next to her.

"Yes, but I have plans that my smart car couldn't accommodate." She slid her hand under his shirt, feeling the sharp intake of his breath.

"Why, Mrs. Barnes, are you trying to take advantage of me?"

She looked into his eyes, a demure smile tugging her lips. "Perhaps. Is it working?"

"Hell, yes!" Joe pushed the button that closed the privacy partition.

He kissed her with all the love and passion he felt in his heart. Her body pressed tight against him, igniting flames that slowly licked through his body. Her hands and lips produced sensations that no other woman had ever, or would ever be able to copy. This was the woman that he loved and nothing felt more right than making love to her, even if it happened to be in the back of a limo.

Chapter 17

An officer brought Richard into the room, where Tom and Burt were waiting.

"Gentleman." Richard nodded as he took a seat.

"Mr. Dillingham." Burt crossed his arms on the table. "I'm going to get right to the point."

"Fine."

"We don't think you killed your daughter."

"We think you're covering for someone else," Tom said.

"Did you search the house again?" Richard asked.

"Yes."

"Then you found the pictures and the handkerchief."

"Right where you told us they'd be." Burt sighed.

"Then what is the problem?"

"The blood on the pictures seems to be only on the back. There is no splatter on the front."

"They're in a pile and dried together. How can you tell where the blood would have splattered?"

"It's amazing what modern technology can do these days."

"Stop your investigation right now." Richard slammed a fist on the table. "You have enough evidence against me."

"You can't order us around Mr. Dillingham," Tom said.

"We want to arrest the real killer," Burt said. "I would think you'd want justice."

"Arresting me is justice." Richard's tone softened. "It's my fault."

"Whatever guilt you're suffering won't go away just because you lock yourself into a jail cell." Burt watched Richard's face tighten. "And, protecting the killer isn't justice for your dead daughter."

Richard snorted. "When did you become a psychologist?"

"If you won't help us, we're just gonna have to catch the killer with someone else's help." Tom leaned his lanky frame against the wall. "Perhaps Joe and Sarah can help?"

"Or Robert," Burt added.

"Leave my family alone," Richard shouted.

"Sorry," Tom said. "It's our job to find the truth."

"I thought your job was to arrest someone for the murder of my daughter." Richard's pale, hazel eyes silently pleaded. "You have me. Leave the rest of my family alone."

"Our job is to arrest the right person." Burt locked eyes with Richard. "My gut is churning, telling me something isn't right. I'm going to keep searching until my gut is satisfied."

"Maybe if you ate something it would feel satisfied." Richard smirked. "Tums will stop the churning."

"All right, on your feet." Tom hauled Richard up. "We're taking a little drive."

"Where?"

"To your house," Burt said. "We got special permission for a little family reunion."

Joe and Sarah sat on the couch, his arm wrapped around her shoulders. Maria and her mother occupied the chairs by the coffee table, and Robert paced in front of the fireplace.

"Dad!" Sarah jumped up and ran to hug him. "What are you doing here?"

"Why have you called us here?" Robert asked.

"We have some business to take care of," Burt said.

"Like what?" Robert strode forward.

"Like arresting a killer," Tom said.

"Then why isn't our lawyer present?" Robert stopped in front of Tom and looked up at him.

"Did you call him?" Tom asked. "It's not our responsibility to call your lawyer."

"If you had told us what this little meeting was about, I would have called him."

"Gentleman, settle down," Burt said. "Mr. Dillingham, please take a seat, Robert you too."

Robert walked over and sat down in an empty chair. Tom uncuffed Richard's hands and he sat down with Sarah next to him.

"We have called you all here so we can get to the bottom of this murder."

"You're already at the bottom, because I killed Mallory," Richard insisted.

"You can say that as much as you want, but the evidence proves otherwise," Tom said.

"Mr. Dillingham, I need you to keep silent while we go over the evidence," Burt instructed. "The reason for this unusual format is that this was the only way the truth could be revealed. We need to have everyone privy to the information at the same time."

"We have people confessing left and right, all because they are trying to protect each other," Tom said.

Sarah's eyes darted to her dad, then to Joe. She licked her lips and rubbed her hands up and down her bare arms.

Mrs. Santiago folded her hands in her lap, and Maria narrowed her dark eyes, willing the policemen to drop dead.

Burt and Tom set up a white board.

"We are going to create a timeline and you all are going to help." Burt used a black marker to write on the board.

"At six o'clock Joe tried to sneak into the house to see Sarah, right?" Burt looked at Joe.

He nodded.

Burt wrote 6:00 p.m. on the board, then placed an X on the left side of the board and labeled it Joe. "Mr. Dillingham, you confronted, Joe, right?"

"Yes."

He then placed an X under Joe's name and labeled it Mr. D. "And, Sarah, you were in your room?"

"Yes."

Burt labeled her X. "Mrs. Santiago where were you at six?"

"I believe I was running some errands."

Burt placed an X to the right of the board. He wrote Mrs. S. – errands.

"All right, that leaves Robert and Maria." He looked at Robert, "Where were you at six o'clock?"

Silence filled the thirty seconds before he cleared his throat. "I was out with Maria."

Sarah gasped, while Mr. Dillingham and Joe stared in surprise.

Robert reached across the space and took Maria's hand. "We've been seeing each other for several years." He looked at his Dad. "I want to marry her."

"What?" Richard's eyes widened. "How could you have been dating behind my back all these years?"

"I didn't think you'd approve." He shrugged his shoulders. "We've been friends for years. As a matter of fact, she'd always been more like a little sister to me, but somehow, along the way, I fell in love with her."

"As touching as this is, we need to move on," Tom said. "So, you two are off over here, cozying up together." Burt placed two X's to the right and labeled them.

Richard wasn't ready to move on yet. "Mrs. Santiago, did you know about them?"

She nodded. "But not until about six months ago."

"So, you two kept this a secret from everyone, including your parents?" Richard's tone was soft, not harsh, sounding more hurt than angry.

"We thought it was best that way." Robert looked at his dad. "We planned on telling you when the time was right."

"And when would that be? Sometime before the wedding?" Richard's voice rose and everyone grew silent.

"Oh, c'mon, Dad, you don't think I knew what would happen if I came home and told you I'd fallen in love with our maid? You would have tried to break us up."

"You don't know that. How shallow do you think I am?"

"Shallow enough to criticize Joe for not being good enough for Sarah."

Richard opened his mouth to deny it, but stopped. The truth stared him in the face. He couldn't honestly deny it.

"I never meant that Joe wasn't good enough for Sarah. He's honest and works hard. He'd made a good name for himself in the oil business long before he started working for me. He has the respect and loyalty of the crews on the rigs."

"Then why did you hate him so much after he married Sarah?" Robert asked.

"I never hated him. But I was upset at how they snuck off to get married. They hadn't been dating long and I felt the marriage was hasty. The only reason I could think of for such a quick wedding that didn't involve pregnancy was that he wanted a way to our money."

"Wouldn't you have thought the same thing about Maria?" Robert asked.

"No. Maria is like daughter to me."

Richard looked over at Joe. "I'm sorry I've been hard on you. I never gave you the benefit of doubt. I see how much you love Sarah, and I'm truly sorry."

Tom started to interrupt again, but Burt held up his hand, stopping him. When Tom gave a puzzled look, Burt whispered, "Let them go. They need to air their feelings and we aren't going to get anywhere with our investigation until they're done. Just be patient, besides, they may help our case."

Tom shook his head, but let the conversation continue.

After Joe accepted Richard's apology, Sarah retold the story of how Joe suggested a prenuptial agreement and she insisted against it because she trusted him.

"Even now?" Richard asked. "After everything that's happened. Do you still trust him?"

"I do." Sarah looked at Joe. "It hasn't been easy. Broken hearts take a while to mend, but I love him and I've forgiven him." She looked at her dad. "People make mistakes. You can't throw away years of happiness for one mistake."

"I know, Princess." Richard hugged her close. "You are more like your mother every day." He looked at Joe. "I'm sorry for my mistakes too."

"What mistakes?" Joe's blond brows furrowed.

"When I found out about your affair with Mallory, and I saw how much you'd hurt Sarah, I was angrier than a viper."

"I recall that," Joe stated.

"I let that anger take hold and I did something awful." Richard's gray head lowered. "I tried to set you up for Mallory's murder."

"Dad, you don't have to say anything." Sarah reached out to hold his hand.

"Yes, I do." Richard looked over at Joe. "I need your forgiveness."

"I don't understand." Joe shook his head.

"I walked into the kitchen and found Mallory." Richard's voice lowered. "She was laying there in a pool of blood with a knife sticking out of her chest. I knew she was dead, but I still bent down to check her pulse.

"Pictures of you and her were strewn around her head. I gathered up the pictures and used my hand-kerchief to wipe off any fingerprints on the knife, then, I hid the pictures in my room and came back down stairs with the intention of calling the police. I heard you coming in and it fit perfectly into my plan. So, I waited, hoping you'd leave enough evidence to incriminate yourself."

Richard looked at Joe. His stone faced expression hard to read.

"Apparently, your plan worked. I was the prime suspect. Why did you confess?" Joe wanted to know.

"I realized I had been wrong about you. I saw how much Sarah loved you. And, I knew you were willing to give up your freedom to protect her. That could only be true love. The same kind of love I felt for my wife. It seemed wrong to keep you two apart, so I said I killed Mallory. Besides, I'm an old man and you have your whole life ahead of you."

"But you didn't kill your daughter, did you, Mr. Dillingham?" Tom broke in.

"No."

"I don't understand why you wiped the handle of the knife," Tom said.

"In case Joe's fingerprints weren't on it," Richard responded.

"Why pick up the pictures? That would have led us right to Joe," Tom stated.

"It also could have led us to another suspect," Burt added. "The same motive Joe had for killing Mallory, also applies to Sarah."

Sarah stared at the detectives. Confusion and doubt clouding her hazel eyes.

Joe jumped up. "She didn't do it, I did."

"No you didn't," Burt said. "I understand you want to protect your wife, but you didn't kill Mallory."

"Yes I did," he insisted.

"Please, sit down and let us finish our timeline," Tom added.

"I have no alibi." Joe stared at the detectives. "You can mark all the X's you want on that board and it won't change anything."

"Joe, let them continue." Sarah looked up at him with pleading eyes.

"I can't." Joe choked on a sob. "I won't let them ..." he paused, tears filling his eyes. "I just can't."

"Sarah, why don't you tell us what really happened?" Burt's kind gray eyes implored her to let the truth be revealed.

"I ... I did it." Her voice sounded small. "I don't know what happened. One second we were fighting and the next she was laying on the floor." Sarah shook her head. "I don't remember all the details."

"No." Joe stood hard against the truth. "I killed her."

"You can't protect me any longer, neither can Dad." Sarah reached up, laying her hand on his forearm. "I have to face up to what I did."

Joe sank down onto the sofa.

Sarah's eyes shimmered with tears as she looked back to the detectives. "I heard Joe arguing with my dad. I waited until he left, then I went to get a drink. I'd taken a sedative and I felt it kicking in." She stopped, choking back a sob. "It had been such a difficult day and I just didn't want to deal with any more emotional baggage."

"I was emotional baggage?" Joe's voice rang with sadness.

She nodded her head. "Do you have any idea how hard it was to bury the baby I'd carried for over six months?"

"Yes, I do understand." Joe reached over and wiped the tears off her cheeks. "She was my child too."

"But you didn't feel her move and kick."

"But I loved her."

"I know." Sarah looked down at her folded hands. "But, at the time, I felt like it had been your fault that my baby died. If you hadn't had that affair with Mallory," she stopped, more tears spilling down her face.

"I know." Joe sighed. "I take full responsibility for everything." He looked at the police. "Can't you just arrest me and be done with this game?"

"It's not a game," Tom informed him. "We have to arrest the real killer."

"No, Joe. You can't fix this." Sarah cupped his face. "I love you for wanting to take the blame for me, but it's not right. I've forgiven you. I'm only trying to explain my emotions on that day."

Looking at Burt, she continued. "I was getting a glass down when Mallory came in the back door. I couldn't believe she had the audacity to show her face on the day of my daughter's funeral." Sarah's gentle face twisted into hatred. "She killed my baby and slept with my husband. She'd taken everything I loved and then stood there accusing me of hurting her. She said that I took our mom away from her, that I deserved everything that happened to me.

"So much anger boiled inside of me. I felt tired and scared. My life had been torn apart and I didn't know how to put it back together." Sarah's back stiffened. "I wouldn't allow her to continue saying it was my fault. She wasn't going to get away with what she did to me. I threw the glass at her as she started walking away."

A slight smile touched her lips. "You should have seen the rage in her eyes, when that glass shattered on her head. It hit her so hard that she stumbled against the counter. She started yelling at me, I don't even remember what she said. I must have blacked out or something, because the next thing I remember, the knife was in my hand and I stabbed her."

She sobbed into her hands. "I didn't want to kill her. I only wanted her to pay for what she'd done."

"Sarah, how many times did you stab her?" Burt asked.

"Once."

"Are you sure?"

Sarah's head snapped up. "I ... I think so. Why?"

"Because, even though you did stab your sister, I don't believe you killed her," Burt said.

"But ... I don't understand." Sarah eyes crinkled in confusion.

"Mallory was stabbed three times," Tom explained.

"But, as I said, I don't remember everything. Maybe I did stab her more than once." Tears spilled down her cheeks. "I truly don't remember."

"Or, maybe someone else killed your sister after you left."

"What?" Joe and Richard said at the same time.

"One wound had been inflicted while the victim was standing. It hadn't been deep enough or low enough to kill her," Burt explained. "The other two wounds were at an angle that suggests they were inflicted while the victim was lying down."

"Then who killed her?" Sarah asked.

"That is what we're trying to find out," Tom smiled. "Now, if everyone can stop confessing, we may be able to get to the truth."

"How do you know that Sarah didn't stab Mallory while standing then after Mallory fell, she stabbed her two more times?" Maria narrowed her dark eyes. "She just said she didn't remember how many times she stabbed Mallory. And, God knows, she had more than enough reasons to kill her."

"That is true," Burt said. "Why don't we finish our timeline and see what develops?" He turned back to the white board. "Okay, Sarah, after you stabbed your sister, where did you go?"

"I went back to my room."

"In your earlier statement you said you changed clothes then washed them, right?" Tom leaned against the wall, crossing his arms.

"That's correct." Sarah looked down at her folder hands, resting in her lap.

"So, how long did all of this take?" Burt looked at Sarah. "Around what time did you get back to your room?"

"I'd say around seven."

Burt wrote 7:00 p.m. on the board then placed an X on the left side, labeling it Sarah.

"Mrs. Santiago where you back yet?"

"Yes. I came back around six-thirty or so."

"I saw her SUV in the driveway," Sarah said. "I remember now because I was scared she would find out I wasn't in my room."

Burt looked at Mrs. Santiago. "You said you didn't go into the kitchen."

"No, I didn't. I used the sidewalk that leads to the laundry room. I had dry cleaning and didn't want to carry it the long way through the house."

"So, you drop off the laundry then what?" Tom asked.

"I went to check on Sarah. I had her sedatives, but she was already sleeping."

Burt looked at Sarah.

"I wasn't sleeping. I'd barely got into my room when I heard her coming. I jumped in bed and pretended to be asleep."

"Where did you go next?" Burt poised his marker.

"I went to my room," Mrs. Santiago said.

He marked and labeled the X for Mrs. S.

"And you heard nothing from the kitchen?" Tom looked skeptical.

"No. I told you I took a sedative myself and was out."

"Mr. Dillingham, where were you at seven?"

"In my study."

Burt placed and labeled his X on the left of the board.

"Robert?"

"I dropped Maria off and went back to my office." He ran a hand through his hair. "I already told you this.

"I know, but we need the information again." Burt placed one X on the right. "So, Maria was back here." He marked the X on the left and labeled it Maria.

"Joe, you were at the lake, correct?"

"Yes."

His X was placed to the right.

"By seven everyone was here except Joe and Robert." Burt pointed to the two X's on the right side of the board.

"Now, Maria, we know where everyone was except you." Tom's blue eyes pierced through her.

"I already told you. I did some chores then went to bed."

"What chores?" Burt asked.

"You want me to give you a list?" Her dark eyes narrowed. "That's insane. I don't remember every tiny detail."

"Perhaps you can remember the big details." Tom stared her down. "Your mother gave us a list of her chores." He turned his attention to her mother, and flipped his notebook open. "It says here, you cleaned the living room and the dining room, loaded the dishwasher and cleaned two bathrooms."

"Yes," Mrs. Santiago said.

"Did you leave to do your errands after you finished cleaning?"

"Yes."

"Did you use rubber gloves when you cleaned?" Tom asked.

"Of course."

"Where did you put your gloves when you were done cleaning?"

"I ... I don't remember." Mrs. Santiago looked at the floor, her eyes tracing the pattern in the area rug.

"Really?" Tom asked. "Because earlier you said," he flipped a few more pages in his notebook, "that you left them in the kitchen the sink to dry."

"What does any of this have to do with catching a killer?" Maria interrupted and threw her hands up in the air. "So what if my memory isn't as good as my mother's. And so what if she doesn't remember what she did with her gloves?"

"The point is, Maria, the gloves were missing by the time Mallory's body was found."

"So?" She flopped back into the chair, crossing her arms over her chest.

"We think the killer wore the gloves when she killed Mallory." Burt put his marker to the board.

"How do you know the killer is a woman?" Robert asked.

"A man's hand wouldn't fit into the gloves," Tom said. "Not to mention, I don't think a man would have stopped to put on rubber gloves in the first place."

"How do you know the killer was wearing those gloves?" Richard's bushy gray brows crinkled together.

"The chemicals from the bathroom cleaner were found on the handle of the knife," Burt said.

"And Luminol found traces of blood in Mrs. Santiago's SUV," Tom added.

"What!" Richard jumped off the couch. "There's no way in hell, Mrs. Santiago did this. She practically raised these children."

Maria sat forward. "Mom didn't do it."

"I'm afraid the evidence is there." Burt placed an X on the left side of the board. "Of course, we still haven't determined your exact whereabouts, Maria."

"You think I did this?"

"You had a rash on your hands from the gloves."

"I told you I had to use regular ones and that happens."

"You also said that you ran out of your special gloves, yet when we searched the house we found a closet full of your gloves."

"So, more came in after the murder."

"We found the invoice. The gloves were ordered two months ago."

"That doesn't prove anything," she huffed.

"You can't be serious." Robert looked at her. "You think Maria did it?"

"One of you killed Mallory," Tom said

"No way!" Richard shook his head. "This is crazy."

"Mrs. Santiago. We've heard evidence that your SUV was parked in the drive around seven. But, when Joe came back at eleven it was parked on the street. Can you explain why?"

Mrs. Santiago shook her head. "There is only one reason." Tears spilled out of her eyes. "But I can't say it. I can't even think of it."

"Mrs. Santiago, did you kill Mallory Dillingham?" Burt asked.

"Y ... yes," she stammered.

"Why?" Richard looked like someone had kicked him in the gut.

"No!" Maria jumped up. "She didn't do it. She's lying," Maria screamed. "Tell them Mama. Tell them you're lying."

"Why would she lie?" Tom asked.

"To protect me." Maria sank down in the chair, crying in her hands. "To protect me."

As comprehension dawned on Robert, he looked at Maria. "No." He stood slowly, numbly. "Tell me you didn't."

"I didn't mean to," she sobbed. "But she wouldn't leave us alone."

"You killed my sister?" Robert squeezed his eyes shut. The pain registering around the corners of his eyes and mouth.

"Why do you even care?" Maria looked up. "She was trying to destroy us. I couldn't let her do that. I love you too much to let anyone interfere."

"Killing someone isn't love, its obsession," Robert stared at Maria. "You were going to let someone else take the blame for your crime?"

"You don't understand," Maria said. "I came home and went into the kitchen. I found her lying on the floor. I thought she was already dead, but when I bent down to see, she started moaning. She opened her eyes and asked me to help her up."

"So you killed her?" Mrs. Santiago asked. "I don't understand how a daughter I raised could do this."

"Why are you treating me as if I'm the bad person? Mallory destroyed everyone around her. She was a bitch and you're all acting like she was a saint." Maria stood and walked across the room. "Why do any of you care if she's gone? Our lives are better without her."

"Maria." Mrs. Santiago stood on wobbly legs. "Maria." Pain gushed in her voice. "How could you do this?"

Maria wiped the tears away. "I had to, Mama. She hurt so many people and she laughed about it."

"But to ki … kill her." The word stuck in her throat.

"I didn't plan on killing her," Maria defended. "I helped her sit up, even though she called me lazy and useless. I listened to her ranting about Sarah trying to kill her. I ignored her rude remarks about me and you." She looked at her mother.

"But when she started threatening my relationship with Robert, I stopped helping her. I let her slip back down to the floor. She screamed out in pain, "'You stupid idiot, can't you do anything right?'" She tried sitting up again. "'Help me up, but first take this stupid thing out of me. I can't move.'"

"I told her we shouldn't take the knife out. She started calling me names again. I got angrier and angrier. I stood over her, wishing she had died. I didn't move and she started with more insults and threatened to fire both me and mom. I noticed the gloves on the sink. I put them on then walked over to her. I had all intentions of pulling the knife out like she wanted, but ..."

Maria started crying. She took a deep breath and continued. "When she started talking about the pictures of me and Robert, started threatening to break us up again, I just lost it. She pulled the pictures out of her purse and waved them in my face. I slapped them out of her hand. She started yelling at me again and I yanked the knife out and plunged it back in again so fast that she didn't have time to react. Then I did it one more time, just to make sure she was really dead this time."

"What did you do with the pictures?" Burt asked.

"I knew if the police saw them, they'd think me or Robert killed her, so I picked them up and stuffed them into a plastic bag. Then I went upstairs to Mallory's old room. I knew she still had some pictures in her drawer. I found the ones of her and Joe and laid them out around her. I'd hoped that Joe would be blamed for her murder, but I also knew there was a possibility that Sarah might get blamed. I mean she did stab Mallory, so her fingerprints would be on the knife."

"What did you do with the pictures and your bloody clothes? Tom asked.

"I changed then I went outside and realized that mom had blocked my car in. I took her SUV and went down to the alley and burnt everything. I had intended to park back in the driveway but I heard voices and knew that the security guards were doing their rounds, so I parked on the street and hoped I'd be able to sneak back out later, but the opportunity never came."

Maria looked at Robert with pleading eyes. "Don't you see? I did it for us."

Robert walked across the room, enveloping her in his arms. "There was no need to kill her. I wouldn't let anything come between us."

"I'm so sorry," she cried into his shoulder. "I couldn't let her ruin our life."

Mrs. Santiago started to sway and Richard caught her before she fainted.

"Mama." Maria ran to her.

Mrs. Santiago slowly opened her eyes. She reached up and cupped Maria's face. "My dear, dear daughter, do you even understand what you've done?"

"Yes, I do." She sniffed.

"You were so blinded by hatred for Mallory that you became her. You became the one thing you hated most. It is good to love your family, but you must balance it with mercy."

"I'm sorry," Maria sobbed.

"I'm not the one you must seek forgiveness from."

Maria looked up into Richard's eyes.

"I am truly sorry, Mr. Dillingham." Maria stood and looked at Sarah and Joe. "I never meant for any of this to happen."

Sarah came to Maria and hugged her tight. "I understand, believe me."

Burt stepped into the group. "I'm afraid we have to take you in." He took Maria's arm.

She jerked back. "No, don't touch me!"

"Maria Santiago, you are under arrest for the murder of Mallory Dillingham," Tom started with the Miranda rights.

"No! No! No!" Maria screamed, and tried to run out of the room.

Burt caught her and Tom cuffed her hands behind her back.

"Don't take me away, please, don't take me away." Maria fought the detectives.

Robert started to rush forward, but Richard stopped him. "They're doing their job, son."

"I can't let them ..." tears formed in his eyes.

"I know. It hurts me too."

"I can't go to prison," she yelled. "Please don't let them lock me up."

"Dad, we have to do something," Robert pleaded.

Richard looked helplessly at the scene.

"You can't let my child be born in prison," Maria wailed.

Richard froze, his features softened. "Child?" He looked at Robert.

Robert's blue eyes registered shock too. "Baby," he said. As that thought settled into his heart he started to cry. "Dad, stop them. We can't let them take her," he pleaded.

"I won't lose another grandchild," Richard said. "But we have to abide by the law."

"My poor baby," Mrs. Santiago groaned. "Where did I go wrong?"

Richard held her close. "A wise woman once told me that a good parent does the best they can, the choices the child makes are up to them. You are not responsible for this."

Tom and Burt safely secured Maria in a police car, then came back into the house.

"They are taking her to booking. You will want to call a lawyer," Burt said.

"You can bet on it," Richard said. "I'm going to get the best lawyer money can buy."

"I'm sure you will," Tom said.

"It didn't have to end this way," Richard said. "You could have let me stay there."

"We are only doing our job, sir," Burt said.

"As far as we're concerned this case is closed," Tom said. The two detectives walked outside and got into their car.

"Now I've seen it all." Tom smiled. "The man's daughter is killed and he's paying for the lawyer to get the killer off."

"This case is a little strange," Burt remarked. "I don't think too many people will miss Mallory Dillingham."

"Are you saying that people should be killed because they aren't nice?"

"No. I'm saying that life is what you make of it." Burt paused. "In the end, what kind of life you leave behind is what people will remember. If Mallory hadn't hurt so many people, she'd be alive today."

"So, you're saying that it's okay that Maria killed her?"

"Even though Maria made a wrong decision, she's still got more support than the victim." Burt put the car in gear and pulled out onto the street. "What does that tell you?"

"With her behavior and the fact that she's pregnant, she'll more than likely get off with temporary insanity," Tom sighed. "I just don't think that's justice."

"Well, it's not up to us."

"Do you think anything will happen to Sarah?" Tom asked.

"Again, that's up the DA, but I don't think he'd want to waste the taxpayers money on a trial for her."

"Why? She did try to kill her sister."

"For one thing, Dillingham has a lot of influence in this city. And, second, she'd make a very sympathetic defendant. Do you honestly think any juror would convict her after hearing the story of all she went through?"

"Guess not."

"Then it's case closed, my friend. Case closed."

Other books by the Author

Death By Broken Heart
Unforgiving Ghosts
The Unwilling Bride

Available at Amazon, Barnes and Noble and
fine booksellers everywhere.

More from Inknbeans

Emjae Edwards, *You'll Wake Up One Morning*
Annarita Guarnieri, *The Importance of Being Shine*
Jim Burkett, *The Nick West Series*
Susan Wells Bennett, *A Fallow Season*
Rusty Coats, *Out of Touch*
Kitty Sutton, *Mysteries From the Trail of Tears*
Dawn Hood, *Pray and Bring Chocolate*
David Rowinski, *The Book of Complements*
Dorothy Legge, *Poems of Faith and Love*
Kristann Monaghan, *The Running Experiment*
Perle Butcher Lyon, *Rebel Wife*
Eric Pullin, *The Magical Tree*
Hugh Ashton, *The Death of Cardinal Tosca*
Hugh Ashton and Andy Boerger, *Sherlock Ferret and the Missing Necklace*
Jt Sather, *How to Survive When the Bottom Drops Out*
Virginia Czaja, *Get Real*
Jackie Williams, *the Tori-Jean, No! series*
Liam McCaughey, *Collected Werks*
Pico Triano, *Let Sleeping Dogs Lie*
Ey Wade, *Tripping Prince Charming*
R.H. Ramsey, *Just Beneath the Surface*
Donna Dillon, *My Special Christmas Child*
Rose Salsman and Claire Turtlemoon, *The Travis Tales*
Kristina Jackson, *The Fool's Journey*
Robin Bee Owens, *Dabby and Maxie*

Fresh Books Brewed Daily

www.ingramcontent.com/pod-product-compliance
Lightning Source LLC
Chambersburg PA
CBHW070816180626
46818CB00001B/287